NOT SINCE MARK TWAIN

stories

by

Gerald Hausman

Newly Revised

"Not since Mark Twain has a writer presented classic American storytelling so honestly. Hausman is at his best with this collection, truly entertaining."

- Hilary Hemingway, author of *Hemingway in Cuba*

". . . hobo, first class, no class -- it's the boarding of the train that counts. . ."

- Bob Arnold, *American Train Letters*

"And we know: this is only a truce, a swift feast of peace, a perching on earth, a brief huddle."

- Elisavietta Ritchie, *Flying Time*

STAY THIRSTY PRESS
An Imprint of Stay Thirsty Publishing

A Division of

STAY THIRSTY MEDIA, INC.

staythirsty.com

Copyright © 2010-2017 by Gerald Hausman
All Rights Reserved

For information about permission to reproduce selections from this book, write to info@staythirstymedia.com
Atten: Permissions.

Cover photo of Gerald Hausman credit: Stephan R. Leimberg, photographer, and the Amelia Island Book Festival.

ISBN-13: 978-0692907498
ISBN-10: 0692907491
ASIN: B004702C8S (Amazon Digital)

ALSO BY GERALD HAUSMAN

(Partial List)

Gerald Hausman Folklore Collection
(Speaking-Volumes Audio)

The Kebra Nagast: The Lost Bible of Rastafarian Wisdom and Faith from Ethiopia and Jamaica

Three Little Birds
(with Cedella Marley)

The Boy From Nine Miles
(with Cedella Marley)

How Chipmunk Got Tiny Feet: Native American Origin Tales

The Story of Blue Elk

The Image Taker: The Selected Stories and Photographs of Edward S. Curtis

NOT SINCE MARK TWAIN

stories

by

Gerald Hausman

Table of Contents

Storytelling in America 1

Hero's Way 6
    A Real Life Goliath 7
    The Horse of the Navajo 15
    Listener 19
    Ishbish 28
    The Story of Terence Trueblood 41
    Bimini Blue 44

On the Road 53
    Along Came Bob Washington 54
    The Billboard at the End of the World 58
    In and Around Onawa, Iowa 65
    From Esther with Love and Directions 68
    The Railroad Oilfield Cotton Boll Blues 70
    Lady Bug Blues 74

Just for Fun 75

    Big Fat Harry Toe 76

    Time to Call the Dog 78

    A Tree Frog Named Houdini 81

    One Bright Night 86

    The Parrot's Scribe 90

Reflections 100

    Three Guys from Atlantic City 101

    Just Like Geronimo 103

    My Mother and My Father 105

    Open Water Swimming 111

    The Ancient Itch 118

Out of this World 127

    A Visit to Cross Creek 128

    Dead to the World 132

    Man Taken Aboard UFO 138

    Talking Adobe 145

    Let's Not Tell Anyone About This 152

    To the Blue Mountains of Jamaica 158

    Pirate Breath 164

Moments of Truth 171

    Snail 172

    Curandero 187

    The Greatest Novelist to Come Out of Cuba 194

    Tyger, Tyger 199

    A Rose for Charley 212

    Old Ben, Pam Snow, and the Blood of Summer 222

Yarns and Tales 234

    Rattlesnake Pete, Goiter Healer 235

    Sam 241

    The Biggest Barracuda 244

    The Seventh Bridle 250

    Of Lions and Men 253

    The Logger Who Knew Mark Twain 256

Acknowledgements 257

About the Author 259

NOT SINCE MARK TWAIN

Storytelling in America

Stories have always ridden the high winds of America and taken us to the heavens and hells of earth -- but we've loved the medium for what it is -- a change of heart, a momentary break from the mundane, a heartbeat from a different drummer.

An old friend said the other day that people don't die, they just change batteries. That is also the history of the short story in America and it explains what stories, in general, do for the American psyche.

Whatever the story is, it's indicative of change. The last great resurgence of energy in this medium occurred during the 1930s and it has actually been said that certain short stories were like the National Recovery Act. Hearing what others were going through during the last Great Depression was healing for many, and shared stories were part of that healing process.

Today the short story in America is going through yet another experimental evolution. In less than 80 years, we've changed from a more or less regional agronomic-industrial nation to a cybertech, global nation. As we have morphed, so have our stories. They've come right along with us, helter-skelter, and growing shorter and shorter as our attention span for detail lessens on a massive cultural scale. Presently we read short-shorts (like many of the ones in this collection), sudden stories, exploded narratives, blogs and others experimental types of brief fiction.

As we've become a somewhat hyper nation of humans, our quickie-fix stories have come along with us, offering both consolation and damnation, by turns. And while most of the stories in this book were gathered in the old way -- hand-gathered, as it were, by listening to them myself, by attending storytellings, and by just "being there" as we used to say in the sixties, I believe this effort comes from a much older ceremony, one going back to the American craft guilds of the previous century. You have to imagine this -- the saddlemaker, at rest, telling a tale in between stitches, amusing some friends who've stopped by to get their saddles repaired -- or so we might imagine.

Stories "in the olden days" as Joe Medicine Crow says, often came from people who worked with their hands. Joseph Bruchac, the Abenaki storyteller and author, has said that some of his stories came directly from his grandfather. While the elder was working, chopping wood, for instance, he told a story. Maybe something about a chip off the old block. Maybe an aphorism as old as an axe and a chunk of wood. So the story grew out of a work experience, an act of artful labor. And the significant thing here is that someone was watching and listening. Culturally speaking, this does not happen much anymore.

NOT SINCE MARK TWAIN

People are talking, texting, running. But they are not watching and listening like they used to.

My Navajo friend Jay DeGroat once said that stories, in his time, as well as his father's and grandfather's, were told to inform the young people. He remembered his grandfather singing a certain horse song while they were horseback riding together (on the same horse), and he said that, just the other day, he sang that same song, for the first time after fifty years, to his own grandchild.

The question is raised -- are we losing this sense of connectedness? We don't live together, communally, as we once did during our apprenticeship to this great land; we live, if anything, apart. On the move. Heading out. But is this really any different from our foreparents' covered wagon days? Or Johnny Appleseed's spreading his goodwill? Or Jay's grandfather's story of the Navajo Long Walk?

We are a nation on the move, we used to say a couple generations ago.

Not one of us, all of us -- whether by force of circumstance or by choice.

We are nothing if not fluid beings inhabited by a space of mind as well as one of geography. Our compass has always been the human heart; and that, again, is what stories are -- compass readings of the American journey.

Who am I? Where am I going?

Gerald Hausman

These are the focal points of the storyteller-traveler.

Storyteller Larry Littlebird once said "We are all carriers of water in the desert."

And so, you might ask, are the stories in the water? Or are they, metaphorically speaking, the jar itself? How about both?

There is a northwestern coastal tale about Raven who changes himself into a particle of dirt and drops down a smokehole and lands in a large water jar. The world changes as a result of this black-feathered trickster. It gains light, and wisdom.

Water is a good medium for the story because as we know water is always changing. And it has the power to, literally, move mountains.

Meanwhile -- to return to the story as story, we have jokes circulating around the internet, mini-videos celebrating mundane daily events. The story, whether words or pictures or both goes on and on. "It only goes out so it can come back in," Armenian-American poet David Kherdian once said to me in conversation.

For 40 years, I have gathered stories as if my life depended on it. I guess, in the end, it really did.

I became "the listener," listening when people said things they themselves didn't know they were saying. I was the listener hearing words rolling off tongues and ticking off typewriters. I was the listener who saw things as they happened, and scribbled

NOT SINCE MARK TWAIN

them down as they were happening. I am still jotting down notes, picking up vibrations, putting it up so it can come back down, watching it go out so it can come back in.

You have it before your eye.

Eye-and-eye, I-and-I, aye and aye.

All of us with an eye, look up and listen.

Look down, eye the page.

Someone's talking to you.

--Gerald Hausman

Gerald Hausman

Hero's Way

NOT SINCE MARK TWAIN

A Real Life Goliath

As a veteran diver in the Caribbean, I was always having deep water misadventures -- like the octopus that attached itself to my wrist in about five feet of water. As I raised it to the surface to see it better out of water, the desperate animal applied its remaining seven arms to a nearby piece of coral. My snorkel was less than an inch from the surface but the octopus had me ransomed. Life existed one inch above my head, but I couldn't get to it. It was only when I was out of air and stopped struggling that the octopus let me go, and oozed away into the reef. That is background to the story I tell here and one that my Florida neighbor, a spear fisherman, also shared with me. What struck me about his story was the idea that bravery is often foolerly. Genuine bravery occurs when you least expect it, and when, in fact, you're quite oblivious of it. Sometimes heroism happens when you press on; other times when you let go. Once in a while, it happens when you do a little dance all your own.

My dad and I are diving the wreck of the *Marie Roget*, a sunken tanker just a little ways off the island of Andros in the Bahamas. The *Marie's* down about forty feet and to get to her, you snorkel over the coral-heads called *bommies*, until you hit the deeper water where the bottom falls away. Our pale legs, flashing back and forth, must look like bait to whatever's down there, watching. Or so it always seems to me.

The big blue makes me a bit nervous. But why lie? I should say, *a lot nervous!* My dad streaks through the sea, a black neoprene shadow. He cuts through pillars of sunlight that go down into the darkness. I just try to keep up with him. Which is not easy since he's a retired Navy SEAL.

Anyway, pretty soon the water changes color again—to a sort of misty lilac—and the milk-riffled sand spreads out forever, with nothing there—except the hulk of the *Marie Roget.*

A glittering escort of angelfish hovers around the phantom shape of the *Marie.* Close to the broken hull, there are popped-out portholes and all kinds of stuff from the ship. *Marie's* guts are strewn everywhere. One time I found a seaman's vest, hanging off a rusted piece of railing.

Most of the *Marie Roget* broke up in the storm that sunk her back in the mid 30s. But there's still fifteen yards of prow intact, with some of the fo'c'sle, ancient and ochre-colored, and frosted with barnacles. You get a queer feeling in your belly, seeing what's left of the *Marie* as she dreams on in the twilit world of the reef.

Above, near Dad and me, a school of blue tang shivers like sequins. In the flick of an eye, they turn clockwise, counterclockwise. All in unison, like a ballet of birds amid the busted masts and cobweb cables of the *Marie.*

NOT SINCE MARK TWAIN

As I say, you get a strange feeling watching all this. A feeling of doom. Of desperation. Of lives lost. One hundred and twenty, to be exact. Dad checked it in his mariner's survey of the region. The *Marie* went down in the hurricane of 1935 that devastated the Florida Keys. No one was saved. If you listen, amidst the crackles and pops of the ocean, you might hear some long distant echoes. Time-warp reminders of the night the *Marie* lost her bearings and got heeled over against the reef.

On the surface, my dad snaps me out of my reverie with—"I see some grouper down there. Think I'll spear one for supper. Stay up top and keep watch, will you?"

I nod as he cocks his spear gun, and goes down.

This is all ho-hum, just another day in the brine, for him. Wish I could be that cool, but I can't seem to. The other day I dived down to look at a fish trap and it had a moray eel in it. I got down there level with the chicken wire trap-enclosure and that eel, grinning like a wildcat, tried to bite me through the wire. It almost got its head through, too. My face was good and close to the trap, and I swam like hell all the way to shore. I was scared the eel was going to break free and come get me.

Dad was sitting on the dock when I came out, gasping. "What's *that* about?" he asked, "You racing something?"

Shame-faced, I told him.

"What are you going to do when you come face-to-face with something that isn't held back by chicken wire?"

"I don't know."

And I still don't.

But I wish I did.

My worst fear is that I'll never get over being a "fraidy-cat." Dad's a born diver. I don't know what I'm born to do, but I'm pretty sure it doesn't have anything to do with water. But who knows? If I could shake the jitters, maybe.

But, now, I'm watching Dad dive down to the *Marie* where there's a bunch of grouper hanging out. Silver chains of bubbles and fins flicking as he descends. I don't really see anything except some parrotfish.

A moment later, Dad's back with a good-sized gag grouper on the metal stringer clipped to his weight belt. The freshly killed fish is leaking blood. "I'm going to get another," he tells me.

"There's bound to be sharks with that blood you're trailing."

"Have you seen any?" he asks.

"None, so far."

He adjusts his mask; blows it clear.

"Forget the sharks," he advises. "Keep an eye out for one of those silver subs, will ya?"

Silver sub's what we call barracuda. Dad claims he doesn't worry about sharks much, but silver subs are another story. They're really unpredictable. Mind their own business one second--in your face the next. And when a barracuda's in range, it can close distance faster than a shark. Do worse damage in less time, Dad says. One time he had his mask ripped off by a barracuda that was drawn to the shine of the glass.

So I'm treading water, watching for silver subs, and Dad heads back down. The outgoing current's pulling me over the purplish wreck of the *Marie*.

Then, as I'm looking down at Dad, I see something come over him.

The thing's like a shroud, a huge dark tent.

Stingray? Shark?

I don't think either.

I clean my fogged-up mask, snort the water out.

Whatever it is, the thing's six feet long and some six hundred pounds, for a guess.

My heart jumps up into my throat. I'm treading against the current, seeing a horror film that's real!

I've no idea what to do.

The thing starts nosing Dad, pushing him around on the forward deck of the *Marie*.

Then it knocks the spear gun out of Dad's hand. I watch the gun drop lazily to the sandy bottom.

Then it comes to me what the creature is. It's just that I've never seen one so large. Maybe no one has.

Goliath grouper. One of the largest fishes in the sea. Normally friendly. Curious. Unaggressive.

What's with this guy?

All at once, I'm diving down — not knowing what I'm going to do. My heart's galloping, my eyes burning.

That monster's dragging Dad all about the deck. First one way, then another.

I kick harder. I'm there -- now what?

It's hard to see with all the stirred-up gunk, but there's plenty of noise. Lots of *clinking* and *binking*—Dad's weight belt banging against the railing of the *Marie*.

Out of the boiling rust and silt, the flash of a hand.

I grab it hard.

Then an underwater roller coaster ride.

Goliath's gotten rid of Dad, and taken me.

It's got my whole foot, flipper and all, in its huge mouth.

I need air.

Round me, whirling, red starbursts of filament. This, and the great blue lips of the ghastly grouper. I close my eyes and see sparklers-- that's the outer limit, brain-gauge telling me -- get up-and-out, or else --

-- but I can't.

Goliath's mouthing my leg, rubber mouthed monster, taking me in whole.

NOT SINCE MARK TWAIN

I can't see but one thing through the cloud of mire: the mammoth fish's globular eye.

The eye looks worried.

Has it bitten off more than it can chew?

No matter, it's hungry enough to keep lipping and gulping me.

Suddenly, as I jerk my leg—*pook*—Goliath swallows my fin—minus my foot.

I'm out!

The rusty dust storm of the deep starts to clear.

Goliath burps up a part of my swim fin. Then it turns casually aside, as if heading for an appointment, and glides away from the rosy billows of the deck, and in another second, it's gone.

I'm gone, too. Blackness. Numbness. Stillness.

Then I see tiny points of light.

Dad's got his arm around me. We're up top, in the air, in the light.

And I'm alive.

The rest is, as they say, history.

I've got my ragged wet suit and some raspberry-bites all along my right calf. When the doctor treats my wounds, he says, "Can you imagine, son, if a Goliath grouper had teeth like a barracuda?"

Dad replies, "I don't think it would've mattered, Doc. You should've seen him fighting off that monster. He saved my life."

Back home, Dad tells me, "Now you know that being brave doesn't mean *taking chances*. It means *chances taken* -- to save someone else."

"I didn't hesitate, did I, Dad?"

"In that amount of time, a split second, a man can die. No, you didn't wait son, you acted fast, and that's what saved me. I was about dead, you know."

"So was I . . . I guess."

"Good thing your name's David."

"How come?"

"Cause you were up against a real-life Goliath."

NOT SINCE MARK TWAIN

The Horse of the Navajo

This story has been published many times and in various books. Namely The Sun Horse *and* The Gift of the Gila Monster. *The story is also mentioned briefly in* Turtle Island Alphabet *and* The Coyote Bead. *A children's version appears in the picture book anthology* How Chipmunk Got Tiny Feet. *All good versions, but this one I think is the best, as far as showing the character of Jay, the teaching of his father and the Navajo love of the horse.*

It all started when my old friend Jay DeGroat was at the post office. A Navajo horseman, Jay was a keeper of myths told to him by his father, a medicine man, and his grandfather who was hired by the U.S. Cavalry to chase after Geronimo around the middle of the 20th century. Well, Jay was at the post office and an old friend told him, half in jest, "You're no longer mobile, my friend." Meaning that he was no longer a horseman but just a driver of cars, a rider of conveyances.

Jay had had plenty to do with horses in his life. His friend had pricked him where he lived. For, tribally speaking, ancestrally speaking, a Navajo is always, symbolically, on horseback.

Jay explained to me one time how horses got to run fast. He said the reason a horse leaves a butterfly imprint in the sand was because of Caterpillar. When Horse was being fashioned in the first days of life, Caterpillar knew where the flints of power were kept in the mountain. He moved too slowly, though, and so he changed himself into Butterfly, and flew swiftly to the flints. Then he brought the flints and gave them to Horse, who, ever after, could run fast. And that is why a horse print looks like a butterfly's wings, Jay told me.

I have always loved that story; I have always loved all of Jay's stories. Over a thirty year time span, he told me a lot of them. But none are better, I think, than this one I am about to tell you now.

Jay told me he rode his horse to Rainy Butte and went the rest of the way on foot. The climb was much harder than he remembered as a child. Then there were twelve men, a young girl and a boy. Jay was the boy who carried the black water jar. The girl whose name he didn't reveal carried a basket of cornmeal.

Corn Boy

Corn Girl

So goes the ancient myth.

A prayer, a song, a blessing of the earth, a wish for water. The twelve men were the twelve Yei or Holy People. There was a pinetree and sprucetree house up top and from there Jay could

NOT SINCE MARK TWAIN

see the four sacred mountains -- Mount Taylor to the South; Mount Hesperus to the North; Mount Blanco to the east; San Francisco Peaks to the West. These were the borders of the ancient, sacramental Navajo cedar lands.

Jay told me this as if it had happened only days ago, but in fact it had happened when he was very young.

He described the lead singer chanting the songs of rain and how the house made of dawn was constructed so that the roots reached up to the heavens.

For quite a while, Jay did not speak. He savored the memory of this; he let me savor it too.

At last he said --

I went back to Rainy Butte once.

My father said to me, Don't be afraid of what you see up there.

I didn't know what he meant, starting out, but after a while I felt it, more than thought it.

The horse came out of the sun.

A golden horse with a mane of sun rays.

With feet of flint butterflies.

The horse came out of the sun and thundered on the clouds, and then I remembered again what my father had said.

There was a circle of pollen glowing around the horse's head.

The horse had a wildflower hanging from one corner of his mouth.

He galloped right at me. I could feel him coming. The force of his body moving through the morning.

Gerald Hausman

I wondered what he would do to me if he kept coming on.

I took a deep breath, released it, let go of that fear.

The big horse kept coming.

I closed my eyes and the sun horse passed right through me. I opened my eyes and the horse was going down the steep trail to the foot of Rainy Butte.

I saw the golden white of his tail.

I saw a cloud of dust and pollen rising in his passing.

And I felt a gentle rain fall after the horse passed by me.

After that, I was always a horseman.

Always mobile, always just what I was.

And what I am to this day.

Navajo.

NOT SINCE MARK TWAIN

Listener

What if everything that is happening in the world is traceable to our inability to understand what is happening in the world. If there is such a thing as original sin, it's the human capacity to get everything wrong, right from the beginning and all the way up to now, and that's what the old storytellers have been telling us, including the Creek Indians who told this story along with every other tribe on earth. This story was published in my narrative history of the North American Indian, Tunkashila.

In the beginning the Great Maker made the earth a perfect place to live, but Coyote, the mischief maker, came along and spoiled it. First he stole the stars and spilled them across the skies and then he took Water Monster's children out of her cave, the wellspring of the world. This, they say, caused the Great Flood. Tree Frog saw it coming and sang about it to warn the people, but only one of them would listen.

It happened that there were two chiefs in the village by the wellspring of the world. One was named Listener and the other was called Honors Himself. They met before a fire on the edge of the great swamp. Water Monster herself lived not far from there. Already she had sent the water people--snakes and fish and frogs--to scatter the seeds of the coming flood. Singing and dancing of the storm to come, they called upon the cloud people to bring down a terrible rain. But Tree Frog did not join the rest. Though the others sang of death, he sang of life.

The two chiefs sat close to the fire, for the night was wet and cold. "I don't like frogs," Honors Himself said to Listener, and he put his hands over his ears to end the song of Tree Frog.

But Listener liked the song, even though it grated a little on his ears. "I'm going to see why he sings the way he does," Listener remarked. Then he went into the wet woods, found Tree Frog clinging to a branch, and brought him back to the council fire.

"Little one," he asked politely, "Why do you raise your voice above the rest?"

"I sing the prophecy," Tree Frog said.

Honors Himself took Tree Frog and threw him into the fire.

"That was a bad thing," Listener lamented as he fetched the frog out of the flames. Unhurt, Tree Frog seated himself on Listener's lap. Yet, once again, Honors Himself seized the frog and threw him into the flames. Four times this happened and each time Listener pulled him from the fire, the frog said, "A great flood will come and cover the land. Prepare, prepare.

Honors Himself sneered at this, returned to the village and thought no more of it. Nor did he warn any of the people. Listener, however, asked Tree Frog how he should prepare, and the frog answered, "In the time to come, the water will cover the land. Build a raft and tie it with a hickory rope to the tallest water oak in the forest. When the flood comes, you will float into the sky, but the rope will keep you from floating away into the Forever."

Listener did what Tree Frog said. He built the raft and braided the rope. One day Watching Woman, who lived in the village, came to him and asked what he was doing. "I am preparing for the flood," he said. She did not laugh. Nor did she say anything. She just watched. But he saw that her eyes were full of the things he did and there was no judgment in them. He liked this Watching Woman, who just watched.

But when he looked up from his work, she was gone as quietly as she had come. Later Tree Frog came to Listener. He told Listener to put bunches of grass between the cracks of the raft, so the beavers would not nibble away the bark. Listener did this and he tied his raft to the tallest water oak in the forest. Soon the rain came. Then the swamp swelled, the rivers filled, the water rose midway to the trees.

In the village the people grew worried, but Honors Himself told them, "This is nothing, it will soon go away." Yet the water continued to rise and soon the people were clinging to their roofs. Only Listener was safe, riding out the flood on his sturdy raft.

Gerald Hausman

When the floodwater covered even the tallest oak, the people were swept away. But Listener bobbed on the foamy tide and the raft rose to the dome of the sky. There it rested, the hickory rope holding, fast and firm.

Far below, fish flew like birds through the silent, sunken trees. Alligators with giant tails toppled the people's chickee huts, and their drowned corn was visited by salamanders and water serpents. Over cribs stocked with golden ears of corn, the shadow of the slow-moving manatee came and went, passing through the green veils of gloom.

Now the bird people, who had nothing to hang on to, hooked their claws into the bright skin of the sky, and their tails dipped into the floodwater. Hawk's tail was striped with muddy water and the tip of Turkey's tail was flecked with foam, and they have remained that way ever since.

After four days the water started to go down. Tree Frog appeared on Listener's raft. "I have come to tell you what to do after the flood is gone," he said. "You will be all alone in the mud of the new world, but do not fear."

Listener felt lonely already, for he believed himself to be the only two-legged person left on earth. "What shall I do?" Listener asked.

"Remember your name," Tree Frog answered before he hopped off the raft and swam away.

NOT SINCE MARK TWAIN

When the water was gone, Listener looked at the mud-glazed land. The sky was grey and dark and the earth was covered with scars. He heard, then, a whining noise. High-pitched, it seemed to come from everywhere--and nowhere--at the same time. Listener was nearly sick with loneliness, yet he consoled himself by making a small fire from the tinder he carried in a pouch around his neck. Then, with his knife, he shaved pieces of wood off his raft and burned them. The fire was the only bright thing in the surrounding dark.

That night Tree Frog came once again. "How are you, my friend?" he asked. "The world is not the place I once knew," Listener replied. He looked off into the endless night. Stars glittered in the still pools of the desolate land. Otherwise everything looked dead.

"Do not fear," Tree Frog said, "you shall not be by yourself much longer." Then, just as before, he disappeared into the lake of stars, and left only a ripple behind.

Listener heard the whining sound again. It drilled peevishly at his ear. Annoyed, he cried, "Who is there?" and a thin voice wheedled back, "Oh, my husband."

"Where are you?" Listener called to the night wind.

"Here," the voice whined.

Then Listener felt something alight on his arm. It was a person with a long nose, skinny bowlegs, and great gauzy wings.

"Why do you say, Oh, my husband?" Listener asked.

The long-nosed person explained, "Before the great flood, I was a two-legged like yourself. I lived in the village and I dreamed that one day I would marry a chief by the name of Listener."

"That is my name," Listener said.

"And it was you I dreamed about," she answered. "But, now, as you can see, I am changed into Mosquito Woman, and all I want to do is drink your blood."

"What happened to the people?" Listener asked.

"They were turned into starving mosquitoes just like me," she sang.

Listener did not really desire a mosquito wife. He believed that mosquitoes were bad-mannered little people. However, he was terribly lonely. Perhaps, he thought, a mosquito wife is better than no wife at all.

So he told her, "You may stay with me if you wish."

This made Mosquito Woman dance in the air with pleasure, but that night Listener could hardly sleep with the sound of her insistent singing. In the morning when he bathed in the sunlit lake, he was afraid of his reflection; for he was covered with red bites.

"Wife, can this really be me?" he cried.

"It is you, husband," Mosquito Woman said.

The next morning, when he saw his face in the lake, he hardly knew himself. For he looked thin and pale, as if the blood had all run out of him. "Wife," he said, trembling, "there is something wrong with me."

"Are you not well, husband?"

"I feel tired," Listener yawned wearily.

Mosquito Woman said, "Husband, I know what is wrong. Each night before I crawl into your ear to sleep, I drink some of your blood. So I am always well fed, but you, poor husband, you have had nothing to eat at all."

"I am very hungry," Listener told her, "but now I am too weak to catch any food."

"I will get something for you, husband," Mosquito Woman said. Then she dipped her long, hooked nose into the lake and in no time, a fish took hold of it. She danced upwards, whirring her wings, and flipped the fish onto the earth.

"Here, husband. Now you shall eat."

After eating the fish, Listener felt better. But in the morning, he was weak again. "Wife," he said, "you must have drunk too much of my blood--I am so tired."

"Very well. I shall feed you," she replied. Once more Mosquito Woman dipped her long curved nose into the lake, but this time an enormous fish crashed into the air, and swallowed her whole.

Dragging himself to the lake's edge, Listener looked into the water and saw the fish that had just eaten his wife. Furious, he grabbed it by the tail and jerked it into the air. "Fish," he said angrily, "you have killed my wife and now I shall kill you."

"No," said a voice. It was Tree Frog. "Do not kill the woman who has waited and watched over you for you so long."

"What woman?" Listener asked in surprise.

Then the fish gasped, "Husband, do you not see?"

Listener heard Mosquito Woman's voice--but where was it coming from?

Tree Frog said, "Look not on what *is*, but on what is to *be*."

Again, Listener stared at the great silver fish, shining in the morning sun. And, as he watched it, the gleaming scales turned into a glimmering woman. "Husband," the woman asked, "do you like me better now?"

Listener was overcome by the woman's beauty. "I do," he said, "but I loved you before, too. When you went to sleep in my ear, I was no longer alone."

Then Tree Frog said, "She was the one called Watching Woman, who saw you build your raft. Afterwards, she watched over you as only mosquito people do--very closely."

Listener, seeing that it was so, said, "I believe we were meant to be together, Watching Woman."

"From the first day that I watched you, I wanted to go on watching you."

"Why was that?" Listener asked.

"Because you do with your ears what I do with my eyes."

Listener nodded and smiled.

"You are two of a kind," Tree Frog said. "If only the others had listened and watched as you did, and have always done, and will always do."

And so the two of them lived together and had many children, the first ones born into the new world after the great flood. The earth was as good to them as they were good to the earth. And their children were listeners like their father and watchers like their mother, and all of them remember the prophecy of Tree Frog, even to this very day.

Gerald Hausman

Ishbish

Ishbish first appeared in The North American Indian *by Edward S. Curtis. I have here my own version from* The Image Taker: The Selected Stories and Photographs of Edward S. Curtis. *Readers have said that the story is similar in some ways to the Grimm tale of "Snow White". In the Crow story though the little men are moles and the heroine Cornsilk is no less lovely than Snow White and just as trusting of the natural world.*

In the long, long ago, a chief had a beautiful daughter by the name of Cornsilk, who thought herself too good to marry the men of her tribe. Her face was as beautiful as her name, which came from the way that her hair shone, like cornsilk glowing in the sun. Now the chief's daughter had many admirers, all of them young and handsome. Every evening they came and sat under the wild plum trees in front of her tepee. Some played the cedar flute while others brought gifts of sweet-sage and braided horsehair. However, Cornsilk paid little attention to the love notes of the flute and she refused the gifts because, secretly, she wished to marry a man whom everyone thought to be a monster.

To Cornsilk, the name Ishbish was magic. You see, she had been in love with him since she first heard his name some months before. And now, whenever anyone said Ishbish, she felt herself falling dreamily under his spell. That evening she told all of her suitors to leave her alone, which they did; and then she cried herself to sleep.

The next morning her grandmother saw that Cornsilk's eyes were swollen. "Child, are you so taken with Ishbish that you must cry all night?"

"My heart is bad," Cornsilk said, looking into her empty hands. "I want more than anything to meet Ishbish. But no one will tell me where he lives."

The old woman spoke sternly. "Hida, hida. You must never go there. Don't you know that others, just as lovely as you, have gone off to marry Ishbish, and have never returned? Some say that he feeds them to his fathers, the monsters of the water."

Cornsilk listened without alarm. "I cannot help it," she said with downcast eyes. "I love him so."

Her grandmother's lips tightened; she nodded. "I think you are under his spell. If that is the way it is, there is nothing you can do but go to him. Ishbish is evil, but it does not matter. Some things a girl must find out for herself."

For a moment she gazed fondly at her beautiful granddaughter. Then she said, "If you truly love Ishbish, then you should go to him and see for yourself what he is."

Cornsilk's eyes widened and her heart beat fast. "Oh, Grandmother, tell me at once where he lives and I will go there."

The old woman sighed. "Make no mistake," she warned, "your troubles are not over. They have just begun."

"But Grandmother, how do you know?"

"I was young once," she said; and would say no more. Then she told Cornsilk where Ishbish had his lodge and how she could find it by herself.

"It is toward the rising sun," the old woman said. "Before you get there, you will see a hill. In a little canyon overgrown with wild roses, you will find a family of old women who will help you. Here, take this magic ball and this old root digger of mine. When you kick the ball, its quickness shall be yours. The root digger will also come in handy. But now you must go, child. May the Great Mystery watch over your journey."

So Cornsilk took with her only the things her grandmother had given her: the ball made of buffalo hide; the root digger made of ironwood. She put on her finest dress fashioned of mountain sheepskin and embroidered with red and blue porcupine quills. On her feet she wore her best elk-soled moccasins, the ones with flowering beads over the front. Then, packing only enough pemmican for her trip, she climbed the high hill that overlooked the camp of her father.

At first, seeing the beauty of the camp, she was sorrowful. The great ring of lodges, over which her father was chief, spread out as far as the circle of sunlight, and as far as the eye could travel.

NOT SINCE MARK TWAIN

Cornsilk thought, "Now I am to leave my home and go on a long journey to marry a man that I have never met." Her heart was heavy when she realized she might never see her home again. It was then that the great circle of lodges, surrounded by the greater circle of the sun and roundly held by the embracing earth, seemed so dear to her that her eyes moistened with tears. Yet she fought them back, for even now, in her sadness, her desire to be beside Ishbish was strong.

After four days Cornsilk came to the canyon of wild roses. They were lovely to look at, blush red and softly whitened by the ashes of many fires. Below the pink haze of the roses, down in a small hollow there was a little lodge, just as her grandmother had said. When Cornsilk came up to it, she was met by the old women who dwelt there; they were blind folk, mole people. One of the oldest, leaning on a stick of dwarf oak, came forward.

"Child," the old woman spoke, "we have been waiting for you."

Cornsilk said, "I have walked a long way."

"Why," the old woman asked, "did you not use the ball given to you by your grandmother?"

"I did not want to miss anything," Cornsilk said. But right away she knew this was untrue. "I was afraid," she added truthfully, "afraid of what might lie ahead. But seeing you here, just as Grandmother told me, I feel better."

The old mole person smiled. "It is good," she said. But now you must hurry along, child, you must not keep Ishbish waiting." Then she told Cornsilk everything she needed to know in order to deal with Ishbish.

"Child," she concluded, "Do what I say and no harm can come to you. Now kick the buffalo skin ball and travel across the night to tomorrow morning."

Cornsilk went on her way, feeling much blessed by these old friends of the earth. At the top of the draw, she drew a deep breath and kicked the ball hard. Away it flew into the purple sky and Cornsilk's feet flew as if winged. Far below, the white-bearded prairie grass lay upon the hushed field of the earth.

Now before the coming of morning, Cornsilk touched the buffalo skin ball with her toe. Gently it fell from the sky and arced slowly downwards. Cornsilk followed it, floating like a feather. As soon as she touched upon the soft grass, she saw that she was in a place much like her home. In the four directions lay the lodges of a large camp. "This is the village of Ishbish," she thought.

Then she spied a woman gathering kindling in the dawn light. "Could you tell me where Ishbish's lodge is?" she asked politely. Without looking up, the unhappy woman raised her hand and pointed to a smoke-smudged tepee, which stood on the edge of a red butte overlooking the village. At the bottom of the butte ran a swift stream of white water, twinkling among the black rocks of the broad plain.

NOT SINCE MARK TWAIN

However, though the place was nice, Cornsilk's heart was sad. She thought, "This is not the way I wanted to be greeted on my wedding day--by a grumpy woman." Nor was Ishbish's tepee what she'd imagined. Smoke-rimed and beaten, its tattered flaps ragged in the wind. "Could this really be the home of a chief?" Yet she'd come a long way, there was no turning back now. So Cornsilk swallowed her pride and climbed the steep butte to the home of her future husband.

When she arrived at the top of the cliff, Ishbish was there to meet her. He was handsome. Cornsilk was thrilled. "Perhaps I've not made a bad choice after all," she thought. But Ishbish, though handsome, spoke roughly. "I sent for you long ago," he snapped, "and by now, you've worn my patience."

Cornsilk tried to explain, but Ishbish stalked off, and she didn't see him for the rest of the day. In the evening, he returned, however, and was more friendly. Cornsilk loved the way he looked and she threw her arms around his neck. Ishbish accepted this greeting with a shrug. Then, kneeling by the fire, he ate the rabbit stew she'd made in silence.

The following morning, Cornsilk woke and stirred the embers of the fire. Ishbish was still asleep. His face was in shadow, but when the flames brightened, she gave a little gasp. The face of Ishbish was all worm-eaten. His eyes were sunken in and his lips were sneering.

Then Cornsilk thought of all the handsome men who wanted to marry her. "I thought I was too good for them," she said to herself. A tear fell from her eye and struck a hot stone by the fireside. The tear's hiss startled Ishbish, who sat up, awake. "I will feed you to my fathers for your thoughts," he whispered cruelly.

"How do you know what I am thinking?" Cornsilk asked. But he did not answer her. The worms came out of the holes in his face; they writhed and his mouth parted, showing a thick, pointed tongue. Cornsilk wished, then, that she might be back in the safe embrace of her grandmother.

"You persist in annoying me with your foolish thoughts," Ishbish said. "I was going to throw you over the cliff four days from now. But I see that I'll have to do it now." He jumped up and grabbed Cornsilk's hand. Then he dragged her to the edge of the cliff. Ishbish cried out, "Fathers, here is Cornsilk who thought herself too good to marry the men of her tribe. You have asked for her bones, now I give them to you."

He let go of her hand and gave her a little shove. Cornsilk, turning around, saw that it was too late to get her ball and root digger. Below her the frothing water crashed and the monster fathers danced in the spray. They were scaly old men with the warty heads of snapping turtles. But now Cornsilk heard the voice of a mole person. "Child, look at your feet!"

NOT SINCE MARK TWAIN

Cornsilk looked down and saw a buffalo skull. Beside it there was a tiny hole, out of which peeped the whiskered nose of a mole.

"Stand on the skull!" Ishbish commanded.

But the mole person said, "Kick it over the cliff!"

Cornsilk sent the skull into the air with her foot. The bone-white head struck the water and the monster fathers fell upon it. The morning was filled with a terrible crunching.

Ishbish glared at Cornsilk. "It should have been you."

Then he forced her to the cliff edge. Four times he threw his weight against her, but she was immovable because the mole people had hold of her moccasin strings. At the same time, many more mole people snuck up behind Ishbish, and they ate away at the earth where he stood. The ground gave way, and Ishbish tumbled, head over heels, into the abyss.

When he struck the froth, the monster fathers devoured him. Cornsilk wheeled about, ran into Ishbish's tepee, picking up her ball and digger. As she did so, she noticed four things that belonged to Ishbish. These were a bag of red paint, a porcupine-tail comb, four arrow shafts, and an arrow-straightener. Taking them, Cornsilk left the tepee. Then she kicked the buffalo ball, and followed it into the sky.

At the same time -- in the stream of the monster fathers -- there was much confusion. "Brothers," said the eldest monster, "we have eaten our son!" Hearing this, the other monsters started to choke. "Aggh," they said, "we have swallowed our son." Then they vomited up the different sized pieces of Ishbish: bones, sinews and guts. Parts of him were lying all over the streamside.

Moments later, these ugly pieces drew themselves together, and began moving about--a leg here, a hand there. And so the parts of Ishbish danced back together again. And he hopped about, howling with rage. "Oh but this wicked girl has powerful medicine!" Ishbish cried. "Someone must be helping her -- how could she trick me otherwise?"

"Son, listen to us," the eldest of the monsters said. Ishbish, dripping with blood and crawling with worms, paused to listen as the father told him that Cornsilk had escaped. "Bring her back to us so that we can properly eat her," the eldest monster said.

So Ishbish agreed to this and ran up to his lodge. Straight away, he saw that his medicine pouch was missing. "The wicked girl has stolen my magic." And then he tore off in the direction Cornsilk had gone.

It did not take him long to catch up to her. Near a hillock of locust trees, Ishbish saw the silhouette of Cornsilk's dress. "I will have you now," he vowed, and ran on.

Cornsilk, looking back, saw him coming.

But the medicine power of the ball was losing its strength. Cornsilk was falling lightly to earth. When she settled on the ground, Cornsilk dipped her hand into the stolen pouch and took a pinch of red paint. This she scattered between herself and Ishbish. Immediately, the paint transformed into a dense reddish fog. However, Ishbish knew what this was, and he turned it back into paint that coated the grass and leaves.

Cornsilk, now running, threw Ishbish's arrow-straightener at him. This became a mountain of stone that Ishbish would have to cross. It took him a long time to get to the top and once there, it was no easy thing to get down.

Cornsilk ran on, and while doing so, she threw Ishbish's porcupine-tail comb behind her.

Ishbish, just off the mountain of stone, now met a pine-quilled forest that separated him from Cornsilk. The tree trunks grew so close together, it was nearly impossible for him to pass by them. "I shall catch you yet," he hollered. And he scraped his skin from tree to tree and left many worms in his tracks.

Cornsilk was slowing down. "I can't run anymore," she said to herself. But then she heard a small voice, urging her not to quit. It was one of the mole people, who said, "All is not lost, child, we are still at your side. Look inside your dress once more." She did, and found one of Ishbish's arrow shafts. "Throw it into the air," said the mole.

As soon as the shaft met the sky it spun into a whirlwind. Ishbish was very near but the whirlwind took him and carried him far away. "Quickly, child, run," said the mole. And Cornsilk ran, though less strongly than before. "I can't go on much longer," she said.

But the mole person said, "You've come to a safe place."

Cornsilk looked around. In front of her was a small stone lodge. The door was made of strong wood. "Whoever is there, let me in."

And the door swung wide and Cornsilk went inside.

In the darkness of the lodge, Cornsilk was greeted by eight mole people. They introduced themselves, one at a time.

"I am called Ivak," said the eldest mole person. "I am friend to all and enemy to none."

"You must have powerful medicine," Cornsilk said. "For one who comes now is enemy to all and friend to none."

Ivak laughed. "I have another name," he said proudly. "I am called Greasy Chest by my family."

"Why do you have that name?" Cornsilk questioned.

"From my habit of using a panther's tail to wipe my mouth," he explained.

"Yes," said a second mole, ". . . he dips the tail into his soup--"

"-- and it goes all over his chest," said a third.

Cornsilk observed that all of the moles wore different clothes. Some wore the skin of the skunk, some possum, some weasel and a few had the feathers of birds. But these were happy little men and they laughed at everything they said, and Cornsilk felt good to be among them.

Suddenly, there was a crash at the door. It was like the sound of thunder. "He's come for me," said Cornsilk.

But the mole called Greasy Chest, shook his head. "He won't come in here," he said confidently.

"How can you be sure?" Cornsilk asked.

"Well, because I am going out to meet him," Greasy Chest said.

"Would you dare to fight the evil of Ishbish?"

"Remember my name," Greasy Chest reminded. "--And now let me tell you how to use this--"

Cornsilk looked in her hand and saw that she was still holding on to her grandmother's root digger cane. "Here is what you must do..." Greasy Chest whispered in Cornsilk's ear.

Then he opened the door, stepped outside, and began to fight with Ishbish. The struggle was fierce. From the first, Ishbish had a hard time getting a grip on the little mole. Greasy Chest wriggled away, laughing all the while. Finally, Ishbish seized Greasy Chest, and raising him over his head, threw him to the ground.

But as everyone knows, the earth is a mole's best friend. Greasy Chest rolled around while Ishbish tried to stomp him.

"Where are you, devil mole?"

Ishbish stomped.

"Where are you, slime fur?"

Greasy Chest popped out of Ishbish's shirt.

Whereupon Ishbish began tearing himself to ribbons, until the ribbons of bloody flesh collapsed in a pile.

Cornsilk then did as she was told by Greasy Chest.

She built a fire and dragged Ishbish into it.

The flames ate Ishbish the same way the monster fathers were going to eat Cornsilk. Soon there were only ashes, and a bad smell. Cornsilk got her grandmother's root digger and dug among the ashes until she found a small hard lump. Then she rubbed the lump with some goose grease that the other moles gave her, and as she'd been told to do by the brave little mole named Greasy Chest, she wrapped the slippery lump in a snakeskin.

And the lump grew arms and a long tapered nose and it began to puff out and move this way and that, and a tiny voice made a big noise -- "I killed Ishbish," it said, and the voice belonged to Greasy Chest who now told Cornsilk, "You are our dear sister, and you will always be one of our family. Will you stay with us forever?"

And it happened that Cornsilk said, "Yes, I will."

And she stayed in the small stone lodge with her family of seven mole people until such time as they took leave of her and went away up into the sky. You can see them there now -- we call them the Little Dipper.

NOT SINCE MARK TWAIN

The Story of Terence Trueblood

This is based on a true story. It becomes my version of truth when I let the reader into the mind of a ten-year-old autistic boy whose main companions were a stuffed leopard and pink blanket. How he survived -- lost and alone in a northern Florida swamp -- is still a mystery. But the fact is, he lived. And though he couldn't tell his tale, he could respond to flashcards that told it in images. I have turned the flashcards into poetry and I have used some, if not all, of Terence's favorite phrases. The autism spectrum is a thread that runs in our family. It may be the thing that . . . well, now I'm getting ahead of myself. Go with Terence, you'll figure it out.

I go down river, I float away.
Mommy, Daddy, bye.

I don't know why, the river knows, I go down river.

I see snake pretty snake.
I see spider pretty spider.

I hungry I eat berry lots of berry.

I see fish lots of fish.

Gerald Hausman

Fish nibble my toes.
I lose swimsuit.
I see moon swim river drink moon.

I hear puppy lots of puppy. Long tail puppy teeth. Puppy like my finger. I like puppy. I see big puppy I swim away. Bye bye big puppy.

I see berry lots of berry. I hungry I eat berry.

I see trees moving. I hear trees singing. I get out river. Dirty muddy nice warm I lie in muddy warm say hi to kitty kitty kiss my finger. I like kitty. I see big kitty, I get going.

I see lake big lake. Long fish like me blow big bubble my face. Swimmy night cold. Trees got shirt. I don't got shirt. Trees warm with shirt I cold no shirt.

I cold moon.
I warm sun.

I see bird big white bird. I get going. White bird black leg get going get flying. I not fly. I swim, swimmy. I see fish lots of fish I see bird lots of bird. Fish water bird sky I get going.

NOT SINCE MARK TWAIN

I see hand, I see man hand.

I see man in boat wave hand.

I hold boat talk to man.

Man say hi, I say hi. I say man I see fish lots of fish. Man say get in boat go home now I get in man start boat I go home see Mommy Daddy tell them.

I see fish lots of fish.

Gerald Hausman

Bimini Blue

Some will say this story never happened. But I say it did. Just the way I've told it here too. There is another version, with a slightly different slant that appeared in Lord of the Fantastic: Stories in Honor of Roger Zelazny *edited by Martin H. Greenberg. Roger showed me how to see the unseen. So this story is as much about him as it is about the old master, Ernest Hemingway.*

In 1987 I was invited to do some storytelling at a private school in Sun Valley, Idaho. I left Tesuque, New Mexico, where I lived and drove to Albuquerque's Sunport and from there I boarded an America West flight that took me to Boise, Idaho. In Boise, I rented a compact Ford Tempo and followed Highway 93 to Ketchum, the town where Ernest Hemingway on a summer Sunday in 1961 ended his life with a shotgun blast that was heard round the world.

I'd always liked Hemingway's work, and now, driving through the sugary freshly fallen snows of Idaho, I couldn't help but think about him. This was big country, and Hemingway, a larger-than-life man, had settled himself deeply into it. I wondered how it was going to feel to tell stories in the valley of the old master. There were good places and bad places to tell stories

NOT SINCE MARK TWAIN

and there were of course stories that could not be told in any place on earth and these were reserved for heaven. I knew a few of these elusive ones, had them stored inside my heart and did not tell them to anyone.

As it happened though Ketchum was a fine sunny place to weave Navajo myths and sundry tales of mountain men and monsters and hitchhikers who wanted to be writers. Things went so well that, on the second day of telling, a member of the school board offered to give me a special, private tour of the Hemingway house on the Big Wood River which was presently a Nature Conservancy office. "The house is pretty much as the old man left it," my host, a blue-eyed retiree who had moved to Ketchum for the skiing, explained, winking to let me know that it was well worth the visit -- "It's not a museum you know."

I didn't need any hard-sell to be persuaded to see the inside of Ernest Hemingway's final home. That afternoon I returned to the condo that had been provided as part of my fee. The space seemed grandiose with two bathrooms, an enormous upstairs living room complete with field-stone fireplace, kitchen, sleeping loft, and two downstairs bedrooms. All this for one little storyteller.

The truth is, I celebrate simplicity even on the road and I felt the luxury of the condo was somewhat amusing, if not a little absurd. Truth be known I would tell stories for free and sleep by the side of the road if I had to, if it came to that -- but it didn't, and probably wouldn't. But it had started out that way, and I hadn't forgotten. After lunch, I went for a jog on the road that led up past Hemingway High and then I moved along the open plateau beyond the town of Ketchum, running along the sage flats, but beyond the ski lifts and into the open country that Hemingway loved. Was this the road he liked to walk along with his duck-billed baseball cap and his long trench coat and hunter's boots? I imagined the white beard, the suntanned face, the persona that had all but outstripped the great man's phenomenal writing skill. Hemingway was the archetypal workingman's writer. The guy any guy could read. You didn't find that many women who loved him, or liked him, or even read him any more.

In reality, Hemingway didn't appeal to plumbers or roofers who read books; he was a rich man's writer, with the vocabulary and hunting instinct of the blue-collar workingman. But Hemingway had the unfailing genius of an inventor, and each book he wrote was new, sparkling new, something that hadn't been seen in American prose, something that merged common speech with uncommon clarity, something that verged on poetry. Something akin to the Bible in its sense of prosody and rhythm. All this has been said before and better than I can say it, but there you have it.

There was a bronze bust of Hemingway on a small bluff overlooking the river. I stopped to look at it, musing on the foolishness of such a thing. Afterwards I sat on the hillside on a clump of sun-dried grass, and for the first time since I arrived in Ketchum, I took a really deep breath and settled into the crisp dead grass of the northwest and let myself dream a little. Some pressures of the day leaked away in the warm Ketchum sun and I lay my head on a pillow of soft crinkly grass, and stretched out some more. Once again my meandering thoughts turned to Hemingway. Writing, he had once said, was something that you did privately. I smiled at the thought -- I made my living writing stories on the air, telling tales that would never -- at least by me -- appear on paper. Thinking this, I drifted off and my tired body seemed to float off into the ether.

My old pal and constant storytelling crony, Old Man Coyote, was sitting next to me. I gazed into the yellow pine sap eyes of my mystical and mischievous friend.

"Didn't expect to see you here," I said.

Coyote, sitting on his haunches, forepaws neatly crossed, grinned.

"This day I am merely a messenger," he said, yawning.

"Messenger -- for whom?"

"For the old man over there."

I squinted into the sun.

I looked around.

The big shouldered hills of Ketchum were everywhere, peppered with blue sage, pinto-spotted with snow; but that was all that I saw.

Coyote made a directional motion with his nose.

"Down there, he whispered, "see him?"

Looking towards the riverbank, I saw an old man in baggy trousers, digging like a badger in the side of the hill, pulling out clumps of grass with his bare hands, tossing them over his shoulder.

"It's not here," he mumbled, "not here."

"What's he talking about?" I asked Brother Coyote, who, wrinkling his nose, replied: "He's talking about his head. That's been his obsession, ever since he blasted it off his shoulders in sixty-one."

"Why doesn't somebody tell him his head's still on his shoulders?" I asked Brother Coyote.

Coyote chuckled, wrinkled his nose again, gave me a sagacious sidelong glance. Then, turning away, he said: "He couldn't hear us even if we shouted in his ear. Can't see us either, for that matter."

"Why not?"

"You must be dreaming," Coyote said with a sigh.

"I am dreaming," I said.

I woke up then, body wet with sweat, my left hand trembling.

NOT SINCE MARK TWAIN

That evening, I reviewed the stories I was going to recite the next morning, and lowering the thermostat, turned in early. The queen-sized bed was much too large for a single person; I tossed fitfully, fighting my way to a restless sleep from which I woke suddenly. There were footsteps in the upstairs living room. The heavy oak floors creaked as if some momentous weight was put upon them. The spectral creaking continued, became an almost predictable pacing, back and forth across the length of the room. First one end, then the other.

Nothing was up there that could -- or should -- be up there, I reasoned. I listened to the footfalls for a long time before I stirred, got out of bed, wrapped up in a Pendleton blanket and ascended the staircase to the second floor. The room had a queer smell, an odor of cordite, gunpowder, hanging in the air. Not unpleasant, but quite peculiar, given the situation. On the pine-slab coffee table, I noticed a book lying face down, open like a butterfly. I picked it up. It was a worn brown-leaved copy of *The Green Hills of Africa*.

I read the open passage --

" . . . and when, on the sea, you are alone with it and know that this Gulf Stream you are living with, knowing, learning about, and loving, has moved, as it moves, since before man, and that it has gone by the shoreline of that long, beautiful, unhappy island since before Columbus sighted it . . ."

And turned off the light and went downstairs, smiling. He lives, I said to myself. He lives. Then I dropped the blanket on the bedspread, and fell into the bed like a natural man and went to sleep.

In the morning the school board member showed up and took me to the Hemingway house that was built like a bunker, a two-story cinderblock home situated above the Big Wood River about a mile north of Ketchum. Aspen, cottonwood and spruce hemmed the house, sheltered it, and the river ran below it, and all around were the great bread loaf hills. The house was about as far as you could get from the Cuban farm where the old man had lived out all but the last years of his life, and yet there was something fitting the isolate solidarity of the Big Wood River house.

Inside, it was a hunter's house and it had had all the requisite tanned hides, trophy heads, and memorabilia. There were paintings from the Paris days, *Playboy* magazines dated 1961, old hardbound books, a writing desk with a green-globed desk lamp on top of which hung a slightly soiled duckbill hunting cap.

I examined the book shelves very carefully while my talkative host told me that the limited editions had been packed up and carted off to the Kennedy Library. "You won't find anything of literary value," he said. A little later, I found a small black book of poems by Archibald MacLeish. Inside was a message the poet had written to Hemingway -- while death was inevitable, he said, so were the Odyssean islands beyond our view.

On the way home, flying back on America West through the snow-bearing clouds of Idaho, I had time to think; time to listen to the silence. The silence filled me with an inescapable sense of hope; anything else, I knew, would have been awkward, inadequate. High flying in the clouds I felt the rush of invisible air, and I fell asleep dreaming of the red dirt roads of the Navajo reservation, and I heard again the elder singing the Blessingway Chant, the song that brings the dead back to life, a nine day prayer that blesses all things, returns the unblessed to harmony, returns all, inside and outside, up, down and all around to perfection and peace.

In my dream the fragments of cloud came together like the skull of a battered, head-shot old man. I saw them come together like shards, and when the broken pot of the shattered head was mended, Talking God and Coyote and Black Wind returned the cloud head to the neck-stalk of the old man's body.

In the dream of the jet stream, thirty-thousand feet in the clouds of another world, I viewed the lost shards, the blood and bone of the old man as the intricate traceries flew across the earth, borne by the ant people, and I saw Spider Woman weave the old man's veins into the web of his flesh and all the while I heard the Blessingway and the Holy People came out of the heavens and blessed the old man by sprinkling corn pollen on his forehead and Earth, Lightning, White Corn, Blue Corn, Many-Colored Corn, Man's Rain, Woman's Rain, Rainbow, Thunder, Sun, Spirit Wind, and Dawn brought gifts of sacred eagle feathers, of turquoise and white shell, abalone and jet and they blessed the old unbroken man with these, and offered him the breath of life, which he took through his mouth and through his nostrils and through his feet and he opened his eyes and breathed sunlight into himself, and thus was he made whole and well again. Thus was he restored.

I awoke on the airplane as it was banking to the south, wings gleaming in the sun, the great jet flashing over the earth and arcing down, down into the Gulf Stream light that stretched away forever and I saw the old man fade into the infinite shades of Bimini blue.

NOT SINCE MARK TWAIN

On the Road

Gerald Hausman

Along Came Bob Washington

I have been telling versions of the tale since the day it came to me signed, sealed and delivered with carrot juice by Bob himself. Stories like this come to you only when your ears are open and your heart is deep as an Appalachian spring.

Along came Bob Washington. He has a white beard when he isn't drinking carrot juice to improve his eyesight. Otherwise he resembles Yosemite Sam. You know when he's been at the juice because his beard turns a rusty red orange color. Be that as it may, Bob can't hear a blessed thing; but he has, at almost 90, the steadiest, most sure-footed walk you ever saw on an octogenarian. And he talks the whole time he's walking with you. Once when I was trying to keep up with Bob, I had to shout in his right ear so he could hear me.

"How's the neighborhood?" I yelled.

"Well," Bob yelled back, "John Painter just grew a mango that set a world's record."

"How big?" I bellowed.

"Four pounds, four ounces," he bellowed back.

"That's nice," I shouted. "Say, Bob, how're your raccoons?"

"The mom's got a new baby," he roared.

"She had another baby?"

"No, she found one."

Then he told me about how the raccoon mom with six kits that he'd been feeding at his back door every night had gone out into the woods and picked up a feral kitten, and it was learning how to be a proper raccoon with the rest of the litter.

"She taught that tiny little stray kitten to wash its food in the water dish just like all the others," he hollered.

"Is that so," I hollered back.

By then we had gone way over to Wayback Road and down Ridge Road to Bottlebrush and, well, you get the idea, there was a lot of shouting and walking and talking going on between the two of us.

One day Bob was walking along and he said, "I hear you're some kind of a writer-feller."

I laughed. "I haven't figured out what kind yet."

"Well, I saw one of your books and it reminded me of a writer-feller I once knew by the name of Jesse Stuart. Ever hear of him?"

"I guess so." I chuckled. "He was one of the first writers I really admired as a kid."

Bob's eyes brightened and I swear his beard got redder than a red squirrel. "Old Stuart, now, he was the voice of the hill farms in Kentuck and the mines and loggin' camps in Cumberland County. His stories are a reg'lar folk museum of sorts."

"You knew him?'

"Can't say as I did. Met him, my sister Mary knew him, wrote a book about him."

We came to the bend in the road where the Brazilian pepper trees form a natural archway you have to bend to get under and walk through. Bob went through like the proverbial needle and I followed suit. On the other side the sun shone and the wind was up, and I thought about how so many of our stories in America started out in the Appalachian mountains and how Jesse Stuart was the songster of those hollows and hills. I said to Bob, "One day I'll have to get into the hills over there where you're from and pick up a story or two."

"You do that," he said, "but don't make the mistake of the man that Mr. Stuart told me about."

"What mistake was that?'

Bob shouted his words of caution to the wind which was generally in the direction of my face, and it went like this:

"This old boy went up into the hills where he wasn't wanted looking for a story. He stayed with a friend of ours and they made him quite welcome. He was on his best behavior, that writer was but he knew he was in a place where the Hatfields lived down one road and the McCoys were on another and both were in barking distance of each other. Anyways this made the writer-feller nervous-like and he had himself a Smith and Wesson pistol in his backpack just in case. Slept with it under his pillow where he could get at it if he needed to. Next morning when he opened his eyes, he felt under the pillow for his pistol and it was gone. He looked all over that spare room for it but it wasn't nowhere there. Then he looked at the mirror hanging on the wall and someone had writ on it. One word. And what do you think it was? GIT, it said. That's all, just GIT."

I told Bob I'd never gotten a story with a gun before and I wasn't about to start now.

"Good," he said with a toothless grin. "And now I got to git."

He turned off Cubles Road, and I watched him, cane-tapping down the road, the fastest, red bearded, nearly ninety-year old you ever saw.

Gerald Hausman

The Billboard at the End of the World

I've told this story to an audience only once. Kids wanted to know about hitchhiking. I told them that in the old days I hitchhiked all over the country. It wasn't such a bad way to get around and as I was a teenager without a driver's license, it was usually a reasonable way to go except that we traveled pretty far sometimes, and always, the hitcher paid for the ride by being good company and telling stories. Or else he served the driver by being quiet and listening. It depended on the driver, but it was fun back then in 1960. People were a whole lot nicer. Things in the world were a whole lot safer -- people, cars and roads. Hitchhiking was a good way to learn about life and as I wanted to be a writer, the ways of the open road turned into stories. None so down at heels as this one but there's a moral in there somewhere if I don't miss my guess.

The fog lifted.

The stars pricked through the clouds.

The desolate road lay ahead as far as we could see but at the dim horizon line there was a billboard. This meant that somewhere ahead of us there might, just might, be a town of some consequence.

We had been on the road for a few weeks. Hitching.

NOT SINCE MARK TWAIN

We were tired down to the blisters on our feet. The romance of the open road was dead to us. We were lonely, but not yet tired of our own company, which was the only good thing.

There were the two of us. My cousin Pete and myself. And the third party was of course the road, that interminable tar-faced ribbon of highway, carless and reckless and owned entirely by truckers whose speeds were outrageous. Weeks ago, we'd hit the road with nothing but a ten dollar bill and the clothes on our backs. We'd started out singing This Land is Your Land, but now we were moaning Nobody Knows You When You're Down and Out.

Hours passed.

All of this might seem tangential or trivial but the billboard suddenly turned our journey into a surreal quest to be back home in our own beds. We'd had it.

On we walked, painfully. But the billboard got no closer and sometimes it seemed farther way, flickering on the fuzzy edge of the endless road.

We hurt everywhere.

Our blisters and the billboard were in league with one another; as one hurt, the other beckoned. As one delivered pain, the other promised rest.

The road had done this to us, broken us down.

Gerald Hausman

"What if there's no life anywhere in the universe? What if that sign is the last billboard at the end of the world?" Pete asked.

"Nothing much matters," I said, "except getting there."

Far, far away the billboard flickered in the fog.

We were on a distant planet, Pete and I.

And that billboard was the mother ship, waiting for us.

Our only hope.

It was millions of light years away.

And as we walked, we aged.

We crept on, one step at a time.

And our feet leaked blood, and left damp tracks.

"I'm a hundred," I told Pete.

"I'm a thousand," Pete said.

Towards dawn, the billboard glittered a little less brightly.

At last, we'd actually entered its orbit.

And then -- we stood admiring it.

A brown snowfall of summer moths tickled our necks and arms. They were dying so fast we couldn't count them. The gravel at the foot of the billboard was carpeted with their bodies.

The billboard had but one thing written on it --

-- *Damariscotta, Your Kind of Town*, it said.

"Our kind of town," Pete whispered faithfully.

The actual village lay on the other side of a bridge that veered off to the right and down below the billboard.

Pete walked forward a few steps and patted the giant mantis legs of the billboard. Again he said, "Our kind of town."

At the same time, the billboard expired. Its arc-lamps dimmed, died.

"I see only purple rings," Pete said.

"Same here," I said.

The billboard, dead silent, had nothing to say.

"I'm going to walk into Damarascotta," Pete said.

"Why?"

"We have family there."

I'd forgotten all about that.

But we didn't walk anywhere; we lay down under the billboard and slept for a few hours.

The sun woke us.

We got up, stretched, walked into Damarascotta.

"They don't live here, but they sometimes summer here," Pete told me. "With any luck they'll be home."

"Who are they again?" I asked.

"Ginny and Walter. My father's sister and her husband, and by the way, Ginny can cook."

"How do you know?"

"I've eaten her food before."

"Call them."

We had one quarter between the two of us.

Pete made a payphone call.

By now the birds were singing and the town was awake.

Ginny and Walter were at home.

Pete hung up the phone. "They're coming to get us!"

I considered this while checking the bottoms of my feet. The blisters were broken. My feet looked like raw meat.

"Ginny's going to make us a big breakfast," Pete said, and liking the sound of it, he said it again.

We stood outside in the friendly daylight as the town and watched the kindly town go about its business. Damariscotta had dogs and kids and birds and milkmen and it smelled good, too.

"What kind of breakfast you think Ginny'll cook?" I asked Pete.

"The works," Pete said.

"Gimme an example."

"Well, pretty little sausages, for one. Rashers of bacon, for sure. A dozen eggs scrambled, hotcakes, biscuits, gravy, pitcher of orange juice, coffee, tea, milk and cinnamon buns."

Right about then Walter appeared. He drove up in a sensible Ford station wagon. Walter was soft-spoken, nice as could be, reminding us that Damariscotta was, well, you remember what kind of town.

NOT SINCE MARK TWAIN

We pulled up in front of a gray saltbox fisherman's cottage with a dock right on the river. The kitchen was cozy and all aglow with sunlight and what smelled like heaven's own baked goods, and we hugged Ginny and sat right down as she said to do.

And the legendary breakfast commenced.

We knocked off a tiny juice glass of tomato juice. My stomach grabbed the stuff and sang for more.

"My, you are hungry," Ginny said with a smile. She had beautiful blue eyes and lovely silver hair.

Walter read the Bangor Times, sipped coffee. Every once and a while he flapped the paper. He was smoking a cigarette and the smoke laced the kitchen lazy atmosphere.

Ginny gave Pete and me one hard-boiled egg. The egg was warm not hot. I looked around for the bacon, the sausages, the biscuits and gravy. Must be in the oven. We tapped and shelled the egg and ate it in one bite.

"My, you *are* hungry," Ginny said. "Want anything else?"

We nodded, but after the hard boiled egg there was hot tea.

After the tea, one piece of toast, butter and jam.

Pete and I chewed slowly. Fifty chews per bite of toast. A second toast came, too, but after that, the kitchen seemed to shut down. Or, rather, Ginny shut it down with – "Such a beautiful day, boys. Don't you just treasure the golden days of summer? They're so gorgeous up along the coast. We just love it, don't we, Walter!"

"Sure do," Walter said, well-hidden behind The Bangor News.

That afternoon, Pete and I borrowed a twenty from Walter and we took the Greyhound bus from Damariscotta to Great Barrington, and after that we limped seven miles to Lake Buel where our parents met us and fed us and never stopped saying how skinny we looked. And, today, forty years later, if you should stop by, there's a sign on Pete's door -- *Big Breakfast at Pete's*. Just go in and sit down. It's worth the wait and you won't have to eat again for the rest of the day.

NOT SINCE MARK TWAIN

In and around Onawa, Iowa

Some stories aren't stories at all; they're thoughts strung together. Leading to -- what? A man's name? "What's in a name?" a writer once asked. And what about his aliases, pen names, chosen or made up names? The name Onawa, seeing it and saying it, set all this off trembling on my tongue. Unpublished, this was scribbled by my wife as we drove through Iowa from one storytelling to another in the winter of 2006. I dictated it as I saw it, thought it, and as we drove through Onawa, Iowa, as if in a dream.

White-fronted winter hawks sit tight on hooks of claw very near the Omaha Indian reservation. I came up here to tell some stories and I'm going to do that but meanwhile I'm watching the road signs.

By truck and silo, field of fallow -- this is winter in the midwest and there's nothing funny about this cold, and I am a poor guy from Florida, a Floridian, if there is such a thing, and I doubt there is. But anyway: burnt stalks of harvested corn stick up and look so dead. We drive by a big roadside restaurant advertisement with a thermometer on it, and I say to my wife who's driving, "No, winter hasn't given up out here, it's thirty degrees with the wind chill."

Gerald Hausman

The road peels away as we roll over it and the distant farms would make you think that the people here are as normal as the water they drink. But then out of a brick farmhouse comes a tow headed toddler in a plastic diaper. I disbelieve my eyes. Maybe it's because I'm from Florida.

Maybe not.

I look back -- she's still toddling along out there in the tundra of Iowa.

I stare until I can't see anything but blur on blur and then I write this little poem on the back of an envelope.

The only part of the poem I like are the last two lines.

In the field of frozen dreams,
nothing's ever what it seems

A few miles ahead I see a sign for Persia, Iowa, and that makes me think of my Armenian friend, David Kherdian, so I write him a letter on the same back of envelope that had the bad poem on it.

Dear David: Because of the fact that you're Persian by way of being Armenian, I thought of you today as we go through the town of Persia. If I remember right, your family were makers of doors all the way back to the beginning of Armenian time.

And so it stuck in my head that a certain Turk wouldn't pay for the work your relation did, a creation of excellence like your poetry only fashioned out of the finest wood, and, well, it was good and the carver was stunned when his craft was disgracefully belittled. Whatever reason, now lost in ancestral time, this tight Turk wouldn't pay — and who's to say after so much time why or wherefore. But the door was done, fancy up and swinging wide and your wily relative slyly slammed the ordered, unpaid door in the Turk's ungracious face and then he, your family man, ran off down the street and that's how your name got to be Kherdian...it came from "Khurda-Katchda", which, if I remember rightly, means "door breaker or door stealer" as in your poem, *My Mother Takes My Wife's Side.*

Well, as you know, I believe in open doors -- or no doors. That comes from my Romany relatives in Hungary. But here's to you and the wide road we've shared for forty years --

>   I'm glad you sell poems
>   Light as a feather
>   Instead of doors
>   That keep out the weather.

Gerald Hausman

From Esther with Love and Directions

There are two kinds of people in the world. Those who give good directions, and those who don't. I wrote this down exactly as Esther said it, and as it happened, and I have not shared it with anyone until now. By the way, I give directions just like Esther.

"We're looking forward to your visit and you will be able to find our place as we are just up the road from Corrales—448 turns to Corrales Road, and we are just one block from there."

"Well, okay," I said. "I think I can remember some of that."

Esther plowed right on with some more "directions" -- "So from 25 South take the exit at Bernalillo and pick up 550 which takes you to 528 & Corrales Road or 448. This will be the second stop light after you get on 528, and I believe that's correct just as I said it. Got that?"

I hesitated to say, but I decided I needed to explain I was already lost, but then Esther got rolling again and said, "Now there is a Giant store, gas and short stop type where you turn. Go to the second entrance for River's Edge Number One, which is Canvasback Road, so take a left for one block to Cottontail and then take a right for 6143 which will be on your left."

NOT SINCE MARK TWAIN

There was silence on the line, while I breathed and she did I don't know what because she wasn't doing much breathing that I could hear anyway.

"Got that?" she asked.

"Well, not exactly," I said.

"We're about halfway down the block with a police car on the right and a mean guy who doesn't talk to nobody on the left. There's a big cottontail rabbit that Ben feeds out in front of our house, so you can't possibly miss it."

There was another one of those silences while I thought about Motel Six, and then Esther chimed in with -- "Hey, by the way, if you see a guy with binoculars, hanging his head over the fence, that'll be Ben. He can spot bear and deer all the way over to the Sandias."

I was silent again, imagining the bear and the deer and myself lost in Rio Rancho.

Then Esther said, "Look, if you can't find us, we'll find you."

Gerald Hausman

The Railroad Oil Field Cotton Boll Blues

This little "sudden story" was told to me by a woman in a parking lot at a Mexican restaurant in Clovis, New Mexico, when I was there one year telling stories to children. I love sudden stories -- for the way they spring up on you and take you by surprise. Some have a moral and some don't. This one does.

--My stepdaddy used to say . . .

--Ever time the old Santa Fe roll by on summer nights in the crickety dark I feel the ground swell under me.

--Was he talking about an earthquake?"

--Naw. We were miles and miles from them tracks at that time.

--Well, sir, I was railroadin in Muleshoe, Sudan, Littlefield, Anton and Earth. Drove trucks on old 84 when the morning sun blinded you and the wind pert near cut you in half but the spudnuts at Carla's Café took the sun an wind and road weary blues right outta ya. Know what uh mean?

--I sure do, I sure do.

--Now, let me tell you something else. They called us O'Flaherty. That is until my stepdaddy turned our name into Fleeharty.

--You had that Fleeharty moniker hanging round your neck for the rest of your life?

--Naw. The kids at school turned that into Flea-hardy. They used to sing a little song back then that went like this...

Clickety-clack, clickety-clack
Wore out your welcome
And don't come back, Flea-hardy!

--That waddn't nice.

--Want to know what was under that good ground out by our old house?

--Sure do.

--Well, sir, that same house where my stepdaddy lay awake listening to them crickets stitch up the dark and take it all apart, and stitch it up again, that house, that very one. That's what I'm talking about.

--Well, I've no real idear whar that was.

--Was near here, in Carlsbad.

--Okay.

--So what'd you guess was unnerneath the house?

--Gold?

--Ahl.

--Don't say.

--Do say...ahl.

--Dang.

--An ocean of ahl. Anyways, he sold the place cause he couldn't get no sleep, and he was outta there by the time they drilled an he dint get a dime fer all them rickety-crickety-tickety rights and

NOT SINCE MARK TWAIN

all them nights sittin and lyin and listenin to that black gooey ahl just a-bubblin unnerneath our beds.

Gerald Hausman

Lady Bug Blues

Bob Marley wrote -- "Everything in life has its purpose/find its reason/in every season." But our friend Ernie from Tank lane in Oracabessa, Jamaica, used to say things like this all the time but once, just once, he said...

If old lady bug lights on your arm, that's good luck
and then you spit on her she don't come back, that's more good
But say she returns, well, that's bad luck for sure
you got to remember, after you spit, say, ladybug, ladybug
fly away and don't come back another day.

Well, I don't know nothin about no ladybug ladybug fly away home
business and her house's on fire none a my business.

But when the rain a-fall, it don't fall on one man's
house alone. Bob Marley isn't the only one say that,
we all say that. Bad luck, good luck, you gotta
choose your own luck.

Just For Fun

Gerald Hausman

Big Fat Harry Toe

Big Fat Harry Toe is a tale of missing parts, and there are many just like it. There is "The Man with the Golden Arm", "The Severed Hand", and a number of others I've heard. Ever lost something? Better remember where it is, or was, or might turn up. So this is also a "lost and found" tale. I first heard it around a campfire, and some of you did, too.

Once there was a woman who found a big fat Harry toe in her bean garden. She knew someone named Harry but he wasn't missing his toe, but just in case, she took it home and put it under her pillow, and forgot about it.

That night, when the woman went to bed the wind moaned and groaned, and a voice started wailing, "Who's got my big fat Harry toe?"

The woman was afraid, so she scrooched down underneath the covers of her bed. She shivered and shook, and the wind growled round her house and all the while, the voice was wailing in the wind, "Who's got my big fat Harry toe?"

So the woman pulled the covers tight around her head and she shivered and she shook and she wiggled and she woggled and chattered and smattered, and finally, the wind smashed open the front door of the house. . . and something entered.

NOT SINCE MARK TWAIN

The floor went creeeek, creeeek, crrreeeeeeek and a voice said, "Who's got my big fat Harry toe?"

The woman was way down in the center of the bed with the covers pulled tight around her, and she listened – but she didn't hear anything. The wind was quiet. The night was still. The house was silent. The woman poked her head out from under the covers and – out of the still, silent, quiet darkness she heard a voice say –

Who's

        Got

                My

Big   Fat   Harry   Toe?

YOOOOOOOOOOUUUUU DOOOOOOOO!

Gerald Hausman

Time to Call the Dog

If you've never been on night hunt in the October hills south of somewhere, then you haven't heard the kind of blarney that comes out of grown men using Red Man chewing tobacco and spitting on stumps for narrative emphasis. So -- if you haven't been, here, and there you are. And now you know how real, made-up, fantastical tales come to be born out of waiting for something, virtually anything, to be treed.

When a storyteller calls the dog, he isn't just calling his hound.

If you're out on a hunt sitting under a persimmon tree in the pale moonlight, and it's October and the ground's cool and the air's cooler, and your dogs are off sniffing a trail, and you got nothing better to do than tell a tale, well, then, why don't you tell one?

Anyhow, the tale drags on as the Mason jar is passed from hunter to hunter, and fellow to fellow, and something paler than moonlight is put into the bargain and gone straight to your belly. They say that adds to the storytelling, but that's only a theory.

NOT SINCE MARK TWAIN

Somehow the story tilts a bit, turns too-tall-taley, as you might say. Too windy or bendy, or just too full-a-baloney, as I might say.

Well, that's when it's time to call in the dog.

One time, when I was waiting on my hounds, I saw something I'll never forget. My good faithful old beagle was out there in the field where I could see him and his head was so close to the ground, he was making a nose-furrow. Here comes the pitiful part.

That poor little hound run smack into a scythe that was left out in the field for a century or two, and my little dog cut himself in half.

I'd never seen such a thing, but there's a first time for everything, so I wrapped him up in my canvas coat, and took him back to the farm in my arms.

Darned if that dog didn't lick my hand and tell me with his eyes, he was going to live no matter what. So I used one whole roll of duct tape and instead of sewing him up, I sort of wrapped him up all silver-like.

And that dog, I swear, was good as new.

But for one thing, I'm sorry to say. I'd taped him up all wrong!

I'd mistakenly taped his hind end where his head ought to be and his head where . . . you know.

Well, still and all, that little dog had the force of life in him. And, you know, he could still darn near run forever. Why, he'd start out on one pair of legs, and run until he was tired. Then he'd switch off and run on the other pair until they was plumb wore out, and he'd go on forever, most-like, but I knew that little dog never did get tired. Funny thing, too, I watched him run frontwards and backwards, equally fast and equally good. And he could wag both ends at the same time, or either end, one at a time.

And—guess what?

Both ends of that dog could catch a rabbit just as good.

So, right about now, if you don't say it, I will --

-- Time to call the dog!

NOT SINCE MARK TWAIN

A Tree Frog Named Houdini

"Houdini" appeared in Gulfshore Life magazine and it has hopped off my tongue at schools all over the U.S. This is what one of my storytelling friends, Bert McCarry calls an "Ahh story". See if you say that, or at least think it, at the end.

One summer we had four hurricanes, one right after another. There was Charley, Francis, Ivan and Jeanne.

Worst of the bunch, Charley, was a surprise visitor, and he clobbered us with category five wind force. Charley was a mighty hard puncher but he didn't box us very long, about a half hour altogether. After he left every telephone pole from one end of the island to the other was snapped off like a twig. Everything in our yard was either dead flat or somewhere it shouldn't be. There was an electric hair trimmer stuck in a tree and my basketball backboard was way off at the far end of our lake, and I even saw a carpenter's level driven through a tree trunk and when I told my cousin, he said dryly, "Was it level?"

Well, we'd pretty much seen everything with Charley. We'd seen mullet dancing across the sky and great big, bloated chunks of water congealed like some kind of hair gel skipping away in the wind.

I let the backboard stay where it was. If the bass in our pond wanted to play ball, let them.

The strangest thing though was a little white Cuban tree frog that we found pressed flat against one of our storm shutters. I unbolted the shutter after the storm and Tree Frog was there. Stuck to the aluminum. I thought he was dead. I peeled him off the shutter like a piece of nutty putty. He was alive, and smiling.

Tree Frog's skin color was white as whipped cream. I brought him inside the house and set him on the counter and he hopped into the air and disappeared. We looked all over the kitchen for him. He was nowhere to be seen.

A couple days went by. One morning I moved the coffee maker an inch or two and saw Tree Frog stuck like flypaper to the back of the machine.

From then on, we called him Houdini.

And Houdini lived with us for several months. He was a good little guest and he grew fat eating all the mosquitoes, flies, no-see-ums, lizards, and worms that chanced to slide into the house. There wasn't any power on the island and the whole house was open. At night we lay awake in pools of sweat. Houdini had disappeared by then, and we couldn't find him. We figured maybe he couldn't find himself.

Then one autumn day about two months after the hurricane, I got an invitation to speak at a school in Texas. Lorry and

NOT SINCE MARK TWAIN

I packed to leave. When we were stowing our bags into the trunk of the Honda Accord, I saw a white flash.

Houdini! How did he get in the trunk of the Honda?

I picked him up and gently affixed him to a Shefflera tree. "Stay there," I said, "there's plenty to eat." Houdini's big eyes blinked in the glare of the day and poof he vanished before my eyes. I looked all over for him, but he had jumped into the next dimension. We finished stowing our stuff and hit the road.

Unloading at the airport parking lot, I saw the white flash again.

"Oh, no," I cried. "Not here!"

Houdini was in the trunk glued to Lorry's leather purse. "Where do I put the little guy?" I asked her.

"We can't leave him in the car," she said. "What about over there on that shady oak tree?"

I caught Houdini and put him on an upper branch and as soon as he settled he was gone.

So were we – we were already close to boarding time.

All during that week in Mission, Texas I thought about Houdini. He invaded my dreams with his large liquid eyes and his vampire pale skin and his great gluey toes. I missed him the same way you miss a dog pal. It was impossible not to wonder if he could survive the heat of the tarmac and the scream of the planes.

We got home to Fort Myers in the dark. Tired and hot, we put our bags down by the side of the Honda. Unlatching the trunk, I peered in. My heart sank. Houdini wasn't there. I searched the bottom of the car and the interior and then I shined my flash all over the oak tree. An airport cop caught me as I climbed onto the first limb. "What do you think you're doing?" he asked.

Lorry explained, and the cop turned his beam on her. Illumined, she told the tale of the disappearing tree frog named Houdini.

This was one soft-hearted policeman, let me tell you, because he got up in the tree with me and we both climbed around and I even heard him call out, "Houdini" a few times. But there was no Houdini in that oak tree. We parted friends. Sadly, I said, "He made it through Hurricane Charley, but I guess he couldn't take Southwest Florida International Airport."

"Hey," the policeman said, "he's a tree frog. He knows better than we do how to live through a bad situation. Go home and get some sleep."

We drove directly home to Pine Island, not stopping at Starbuck's as we usually do. At home, our two dogs, Great Dane Zora and Dachshund, Mousie, greeted us with wet noses and kisses, and after we put our bags on the bench by the door, we went right to bed.

NOT SINCE MARK TWAIN

I dreamed all night of unimaginable things. Hot, sweaty dreams of being lost on planets of no mercy where water looked like mercury and long tapered, upright beings spoke to me through their eyes, which were the eyes of tree frogs. "I'm alive and well," one of these creatures said with his bulbous and burny eyes.

"Where?" I asked with my own eyes.

"Look for me," the eyes said. "Look for me."

In the morning, I went out to the Honda.

"This is nuts," I said to Lorry.

"What harm?" she asked.

"None, I guess."

I lifted the trunk. It was already hot in there and it smelled like scorched plastic.

I saw the white flash. So did Lorry.

Then a soundless sound as a weightless weight traversed space and time.

Alighting -- poit! -- on my right forearm.

"Good little tree frog," Lorry said.

"Good little Houdini," I said.

Gerald Hausman

One Bright Night

There is an Anglo-Saxon form of riddling that plays with the polarities of words like bright and dark, cold and warm, throwing them against one another and crafting lines of rich, humorous nonsense like this poem that has been around for so many hundreds of years that you just have to sit back and, with nothing else in mind, laugh out loud.

One bright night in the middle of the day
I saw a bald baby with hair all gray
He said he was a papa but I thought he was my mum
He ground his teeth but he hadn't got one
He sat all pretty and he talked up a song
It wasn't very short and it wasn't very long --
One fine day in the middle of the night
Two dead boys had a fight
Back-to-back they faced each other
Drew their swords and shot each other.

    I recited this once at a school visit and a girl raised her hand and I called on her and she said –
    "My father says that one to me before I go to sleep, and there's more to it and it goes like this --

NOT SINCE MARK TWAIN

One fine day in the middle of the night
Two dead boys got up to fight
Back-to-back they faced each other
Pulled their swords and shot each other.
The deaf policeman heard the noise
Came and shot the two dead boys
If you don't believe this lie is true
ask the blind man, he saw it too.

Who knows how far this tale goes back; I've read that the earliest manuscript verse is from 1305. It's tangled up, this history, but the words are always fun to kick around on the tongue. There's more, by the way. A bit of research turned up this --

A paralyzed donkey was passing by
And kicked the blindman in the eye
Knocked him through a nine inch wall
Into a dry ditch and drowned them all.

Usually, when I am visiting a school and riddling the kids with tangletalk, they ask for more. Sometimes I give them the story-in-the-round that my grandfather used to say to me when I was five.

"It was a dark and stormy night
Robbers were gathered round the fire
The oldest of them said, "Tell me a story.
The youngest said, "It was a dark and stormy night,
Robbers were gathered
Round the fire, the oldest of them said…"

Another of these old poems comes from Iceland and I used it recently in a "riddling contest" at a school in Highland, Texas. "Tell me," I said, "who are *the two* and what is *the Thing*. If you can give me the answer by the end of the day, I'll give you a free book." Well, of course these twenty-first century kids needed a tenth century Icelandic clue. I gave it to them and by day's end, one boy gave me correct answers for both the two and the thing. Here is the riddle poem –

Who are the two who ride to the Thing?
Three eyes they have together
Ten feet and one tail
And thus they travel through the lands.

A little bit of Norse information is useful here and my contest winner went to a book of Norse legends and learned that "the Thing" was a great meeting of early democracy, a sharing of

NOT SINCE MARK TWAIN

policy and mind that covered everything from title disputes to taxes. The god Odin rode to the Thing on an eight-legged horse named Sleipnir (meaning Slipper). Odin had two eyes, Sleipnir had one.

So, a ten-year-old Hispanic boy ferreted out the answer to the riddle. Plus a fantasy writer from Mission, Texas, who answered the same riddle in a cab on the way to the airport. "That wasn't hard," she said. "Not if you have words tripping off your tongue," I said.

Gerald Hausman

The Parrot's Scribe

George the parrot is not normal. I don't know what normal is for a parrot any more than I know what it is for a human. But any parrot that can watch a murder mystery on TV, and then, when the bad guy finally gets what's coming to him, asks -- "Hey, what happened to the man?" I say, "He's dead, George." And George looks me in the eye, and says, "Yeah, sure," real sarcastic-like, yeah, well, any parrot that can do this and always put it in the right context is either not-normal, or just plain super-normal. And I'm not going to add, "for a bird" because that's where we humans get into trouble. George gets into trouble by merely talking. And I readily admit to being the parrot's scribe but not the parrot's press agent. He doesn't need me for that.

A little while ago I watched a flock of conures fly over our house. They're noisy, jittery birds, and I loved them at first sight. Sometimes they hang out in our Shefflera tree. They consume the little black fruits, or seeds, making a glorious big mess the way parrots do. They throw stuff all over the place, then, in a rush of abandonment, they're off in a green whirl to another property where their calls and squalls are heard for a mile or more. I have seen parrot flocks in downtown Fort Lauderdale and I have read about the monk parakeets making unruly nests in Florida and all over the Northeast. Parakeets in Connecticut doesn't sound right somehow, though I've heard they're in Chicago, too.

However, the parrots of Pine Island seem in synchrony with this green heaven of ours—well, probably not if you own a grove or tropical fruit farm, for then it's as my Jamaican friend Roy says, "Parrots are destroyful."

I should know this myself, as I have lived with a contentious Blue-fronted Amazonian parrot for the past twenty-seven years. My daughters are fearful that I will put him in my final will and testament. Neither one wants George. They've made that perfectly clear.

They're not the only ones.

Quite a number of Pine Islanders feel the same way. Even those who don't know George personally have been forced to know him auditorially, so to say.

From time to time, I've dipped into the literature of the parrot seeking answers to various questions about their oddball behavior. We all know jokes about ill-tempered parrots -- but why are they that way?

Is it because the best defense is offense?

Medieval monks, the ones who wrote the first books of natural and unnatural history, which they called bestiaries, had a special point of view when it came to parrots. The monks depicted parrots as indestructible animals. The hardest part of a parrot's body, they said, was its head.

So far, so true. However, the bestiarists went further than that; they wrote that a parrot could dive out of the sky, drop down, and crash on the point of its beak without doing any harm to itself. Maybe the monks meant this metaphysically. In any case, I've seen parrots dive. But I've never seen one stuck in the ground, headfirst. Not that I wouldn't like to…in the case of George.

It's arguably true that a parrot's hard part is his head. George, for instance, is as hardheaded and as loud-mouthed as they come. And, if it's true that he who talks loudest lives longest, well, we should all raise our voices like George, for this very well could be the ultimate source of longevity.

Joking aside, Amazonian parrots, of which George is one, can live 75 years or more. Macaws live longer than that.

Actually, I've stopped thinking of George as a parrot. He is a child. When I roll his cage into the hallway, he cries like a baby, until our guests beg me to wheel him back into range of our dinner. Whereupon he begs for chicken bones—he loves to crack them and suck out the marrow. He loves scrambled eggs, too. Thus making him a cannibal, I suppose. But the words that come out of his beak when he's not screeching for goodies defy the latest avian research.

NOT SINCE MARK TWAIN

The other day when my artist friend John Bredin came over to the house, he stopped in the kitchen to say hello to George. "How are you doing, George?" John said. George looked at John and replied —"Too busy to talk to you now!" He was pacing on his perch when he said it, too, like a man who has no time to waste on idle talk. John gave me a critical glance and commented, "Wonder where he got that."

A day or so after, I was out on our porch waiting for the mail. As William Saroyan once observed, "We are all men of letters waiting for the mail." I was expecting a check, and there I was (probably pacing like George, who was right behind me in his cage) waiting and looking, when the mail lady drove up in her little right-sided Jeep. Cheerfully, I said, as much to myself as to George, "Well, there she is at last." And George replied demurely, "What are you talking about, I can't even see her from here."

The reason I believe George is a thinking being, not just an imitative one is because his remarks are often not repeated. He says what he will, when he will, as he will. And there's no coaxing another epithet or comment like the one he said earlier. He really talks the way we do; he observes things and makes remarks that have substance.

He does, however, repeat "nighty-night" when it's time to go to sleep. But he only says it once when we turn out the lights.

Gerald Hausman

When our incontinent and aged dachshund had an accident on the kitchen floor, I heard George make an audible sigh from his perch, and he said, "The poor little thing." For the rest of that day, my wife and I counseled ourselves on learning to be as compassionate as our parrot.

In addition to his uncanny ability to speak proper English at the proper time, George exhibits other traits that show an uncanny degree of appropriate intelligence. The other day when our carpet was being cleaned by an efficiency expert with a loud voice and a militant manner, George growled at her. This meant, "Pipe down, pal, I don't like your style." When the officious carpet cleaner continued shouting, George slipped out of his cage and flew at her face. She screamed as George alighted in her abundance of auburn, deep pile hair. The poor lady stood perfectly still as I untangled George's claws from her hair. After he was safely ensconced in his cage and the door was locked, the carpet lady said, "People say my voice is grating, and I guess it is. Your parrot thinks so, that's for sure." She was quiet for the rest of that day. George preened his feathers and looked well satisfied with himself.

The worst George attack on record was when he went after a photographer from the News-Press. This affable fellow wanted a picture of the whole family, our animal family, with us in the middle. I warned him, "George doesn't like to have his picture taken." The photographer smiled with indulgence. "I just finished a shoot with some Bengal tigers—you think I'm afraid of a little bird?"

I shrugged, and said, "Have it your way."

George was balanced on my index finger when the photographer snapped his first shot. I tried to hold George back, I really did. But he exploded. He turned into a green meteor. George flew at the man, who used his telephoto lens to ward George's flared claws. I guess the poor fellow got a scratch or two in the encounter, but he was sanguine about it. I put George back in his cage.

"Well," the photographer said, "I didn't believe a parrot was faster than a tiger, but now I know different."

Some neighbors think we should have George's wings and claws clipped. We don't want to do that. What if he needed to fly to escape the hawks that come within range of his cage? I've seen them dive at him. One day I put George outside so he could enjoy a little sunshine. He has a perch on top of his four-wheeler cage. One second he was there talking to me. The next second he was gone. I spent the rest of that day searching for him, with no luck. Our house is surrounded by pine flats and palmettos. Out there the hawks scream and the eagles chortle and the parrots, if there are any out there, lie low to the ground.

My wife and I walked the shell roads repeatedly calling out, "Georgie, Georgie."

But he never answered.

Gerald Hausman

At dusk I went out one last time.

Way off in the palmettos I heard a little, far away voice say, "Hel-loo, hello, hell-ooooo." I yelled, "George!" And he said, "Help!" Just once, but it was plain and clear, and I ran to where I thought I heard the pitiful cry, and there he was crouched low at the base of a slash pine. I really thought he was going to say, "What took you so long?" But he didn't. On the way home, he scrunched himself down flat and had a wary eye trained on the sky. I gave him a little kiss and he said in a small, pathetic voice, "Is that it, then?"

That outing didn't faze him much, or else he completely forgot about it the following day, because he was in his cage on the porch when I heard him giving someone a hard time. I wondered who it could be. Well, we have a wall of trees in front of the house, so it's hard to see into the property. Here was this guy walking his dog and having a spirited conversation with George. He couldn't see George and George couldn't see him, but they certainly could hear one another.

The dog-walking gentleman was saying, "Well, son, you just keep up that foul talk and I'll come over there and wash your mouth out." The outraged man sounded like Foghorn Leghorn. I don't know what George had said to irritate him, but this was an incident in the making. I called through the fence of trees, "You're throwing insults at a bird, sir."

The indignant walker responded, "Give me the bird, and I'll wash both of your mouths out!"

As I wheeled George back into the house, I muttered, "What's wrong with the world is everybody's trying to fix everybody else."

George eyed me with curiosity, and said, for the second time, "Well, that's it, then."

"Yes," I said, "I guess it is."

George chuckled, sounding very much like a frog.

I wheeled him into the kitchen and, well, I hate to admit to a cliché, but I offered him a cracker.

George regarded the saltine with some disdain. Then he gave me a bribed look, and said with sarcasm, "There you go." Snatching the cracker he dropped it into his water dish and turned his back on it

Shortly after this, a telemarketer called with some insidious phone plan. After hanging up, I sighed and said, "What a jerk!"

George flashed a game eye in my direction, and quipped, "You're the jerk!"

It's not surprising to me that an Amazonian parrot can talk as well as George does, but sometimes I wonder why he's such a grouch. Author Eugene Linden explains this, however, in his book *The Parrot's Lament*. "Unlike dogs and cats, domesticated for thousands of years, parrots are wild animals, not at all adapted to human company. Their needs and neuroses are not nearly as well understood as those of other pets, and these smart, highly social animals are capable of making life a living hell if an owner inadvertently presses a hot button."

One such button was pressed the other night at a dinner party here at the house. One of our guests insisted she was especially good with animals and could soothe a raging beast. I told her to beware of George, whose beastliness was beyond normal bounds. Our guest replied, "Oh, he'll be eating out of my hand before the night's over." When George bit her, she cried out in pain, and George promptly asked, "That hurt?"

I was told that night that I should seek a therapist for my aberrant bird. There is such a thing, by the way, as a parrot shrink. One of them is a lady named Sally Blanchard, who is really an animal behaviorist in Alameda, California. I didn't call Sally, though; I phoned a friend of mine, Fred Maas, who has an African Gray. He listened to my tale of George's woes, and said, "I think George needs two places of residence: a daytime house and a nighttime roost. This is consistent with parrot behavior in the Amazon region."

So, feeling Fred's instinct was right, I got George another cage. This one I set up in the small office where I do all of my writing. It gets a bit crowded in here with our Great Dane, Dachsy and Siamese cat—and now, George—but that's the end of the tale. George loves being in the office. He likes to hear the computer keys clicking. His behavior is much less antisocial, too. I suppose he fancies himself the writer of this essay, which isn't all that untrue, come to think of it. Guess that makes me the parrot's scribe. I can live with that.

Gerald Hausman

Reflections

Three Guys from Atlantic City

a play for voices

This little script came to me exactly as I have written it. I was eating breakfast in one of the last great diners on New Jersey's south shore and suddenly these three pundits began their disquisition. I wrote it down as fast as I could and afterwards realized it was, in a sense, a William Saroyan play. Well, almost, anyway.

First Guy: (loudly) Now, when the people went into the Sinai following Moses they walked in the desert for 40 years.

Second Guy: (softly) Forty years? I spent 50 years putting on my shoes this morning. But wasn't it something like 400 years? – I mean *their* time not *ours*.

Third Guy: (whispery) I think it was more like four years, or better yet, four days. By the way, that's how long it's taking us to get our muffins in this diner.

First Guy: They call it the 50-50 diner, y'know why? Cause 50% of what's on the menu isn't available and the other 50% isn't any good.

Second Guy: Hey, I don't mean to change the subject, but what do you guys think of the messiah?

Third Guy: You mean the *film* with that actor, Mel Gibson?

Second Guy: No, I mean the *man*.

First Guy: I think he had *pow-wers*. Leave it at that.

Third Guy: *Before* or *after* he died?

Second Guy: Is there a difference?

First Guy: Powers . . . schmowers. Did I tell ever tell you about Rabbi Shmelke? He heard melodies no human ever heard. He heard singing that wasn't even invented yet!

Third Guy: What melodies? Hey, look, our muffins are here.

Second Guy: I'm in heaven!

First Guy: *Before* or *after* you eat?

NOT SINCE MARK TWAIN

Just Like Geronimo

This happened, and it may be mere reportage of an event of small consequence, but to me, it was of large significance. I'd heard someone saying that Santa Fe was a changed town. That you no longer heard stories spoken on the streets. Well, that's why we came to Santa Fe in the early sixties and why we lived in New Mexico for more than twenty-two years and I'm glad there are still ancient echoes on the Paseo. "Just Like Geronimo" appeared in the booklet Bokeelia, *published by Longhouse Publishers, and it was also included in Full Metal Poem, a magazine published in Germany.*

I was sitting in Dunkin Donuts on the Paseo outside Santa Fe. I used to go there a lot because, no matter what time of day or night, there were storytellers. Just people talking about their lives, in Spanish, English, Tewa, Tiwa, Towa, Navajo and sometimes Apache. I got whole collections of stories from just sitting and listening to people talk.

I knew someone, a student of mine actually, who was a direct descendant of Geronimo but he never talked about the man and he didn't look related, whatever that means, and I only got one story from him about another not-so-famous warrior relation who took about a thousand bullets in the chest and lived. It was one of the best stories I ever read.

Gerald Hausman

So, anyway, one day at Dunkin Donuts there was a man seated at the counter who looked just Geronimo. I seated myself next to him. He was sipping some coffee, no donut and looking straight ahead. Slowly he turned toward me and said straight out of the blue – "Who's your favorite conductor?"

"I haven't been on a train lately."

He cut me with his eyes. "I'm referring to symphonic conductors."

"I don't know," I said.

"With me," he said, "It's a toss up. Eugene Ormandy, Erich Leinsdorf, Arthur Fiedler, or Seiji Ozawa."

"I saw Seiji Ozawa once," I told him.

"Yeah? What'd he look like?"

"Small, intense. Very nice hair."

"Ever see Ormandy?"

"Matter of fact I lived a block away from him."

"What'd he look like?"

"An old man in a heavy overcoat."

"Yeah? Say hello to Ormandy, if you see him again."

"He's dead."

"Nah, he's trodding the earth, just like Geronimo."

NOT SINCE MARK TWAIN

My Mother and My Father

When I first went out on the road as a storyteller, I had a full set of stories, and this was one of them. It hasn't appeared in print; I never tried to write it. But I must've told it a few hundred times. Knowing parents is nothing like explaining them to those who didn't know them. But, then, maybe we don't ever know who our parents are until we finally let go of who we think we are as a result of them.

I have a hard time explaining my parents to people because they, my mom and dad, were sort of unusual. Sometimes I don't think of them as parents but rather as friends, very good friends of my brother and me. Sometimes I see them as lovers, as two who loved each other so deeply that there was no room for anyone else in their life. But of course that is silly, and I know it. Because they made room for my brother and me. Occasionally, I see my mom and dad as they were on the farm in Maryland, in 1946, running naked in the rain, their bodies still young and glistening. I am in the tree house with my brother and it is raining and our parents are naked, holding hands and running across the green grass of that remote hilltop farm.

I think of them that way sometimes.

But it's no good. I might as well see them sitting next to each other in the Quaker Meeting House in Westminster, for they were there too, only clothed. As were my brother and me, also clothed, but none of us have ever had anything against nakedness, which is maybe why I am telling this story. It's about being open and free and loving and going that way full tilt until the end. If there is an end – and that is another reason I'm telling this story. I'm not sure there is an end -- to anything. It only seems that way. But I am getting away from my parents, and I don't want to.

My father always looked like Ernest Hemingway to me. That is, if Hemingway had been a short Hungarian. Well, their mustaches were the same anyway. The other day I showed Hilary Hemingway a picture of my dad and she said, "Are we cousins then?"

My mother resembled, if she liked, Queen Elizabeth, whom she neither liked nor disliked. But there was nothing of the royal air in my mother. She was, however, descended from Mayflower stock and had a certain presence, a way of holding her head and shoulders very erect. Her hands were beautiful, long and tapered. And her eyes.

One time my father said, "I didn't fall in love with her on first sight. It was second and third sight, and after a time I just loved the way she looked, every part of her, every little thing: her face, her hands, her feet. When we first met, I was in love with a woman in the mist. Then, in Mexico, I ran away from her and so doing I ran away from myself. One time, when I was supposed to meet her and give an engagement ring, I got in a canoe instead and paddled on the Chesapeake and got lost and I think I broke her heart a little but I didn't mean to do that. I was confused. I had a funny family and I didn't want her to know about it."

My mother's story of their first meeting was a little different. But she did bring up the part about the mist. They were connected to water, these two, from lake to lake, they met and fell in and out of love, and eventually I scattered their ashes in the lake they loved the most. Ah but I am far ahead of myself.

My mother told me this: "I met your father the summer I was tutoring Gloria Vanderbilt at the Whitney family estate in the Adirondacks of New York State. I would get up in the early morning before anyone else was awake. I would dress and go out on the dock to listen to the loons. That was where I saw your father for the first time. He was canoeing across the lake, which was private. I supposed he did not know that. I saw him from a distance of about thirty feet – a handsome mustached man, very dark of face and hair, and strongly built with very wide shoulders like a gymnast, well, you know he was a gymnast. He waved. I waved back. I said to myself, "If I could have a man like that I wouldn't ever let him go." I was unmarried and, at age 30 I was wondering if…well, that is another story. But your father waved and I waved and then the shrouds of early morning mist closed over the lake front, and the canoeist disappeared. Forever, I thought. Because when the fog went away, the man in the canoe was gone. I wouldn't see him again for ten years."

"Where did you meet him again?"

"I met him in Mexico. Actually, it was on a train going to Veracruz. I saw a dark handsome man with a mustache sitting by himself as the train moved sinuously through the mountains and down to the sea, and I wondered if he would talk to me if I talked to him and whether or not he spoke any English, for I was sure he was Mexican. What a surprise when I did talk to him and he turned out to have a bit of a Brooklyn accent. He, like me, was a New Yorker. And there we were – just like that – sitting together and so deeply in love we almost couldn't speak. But we did speak and I remembered him and he remembered me from that distant morning on that Adirondack lake. And we were so much in love."

I asked my father what he felt on the train and afterwards in Veracruz and he said, "I made a mistake, not the first one, mind you, the first of many, like the time I ran away in the canoe on the Chesapeake when we were supposed to be engaged. The problem, I suppose, was that I felt she was just too good for me. When I found out about her background, her blueblood and all that, I got worried she'd never want anything to do with a crazy bunch of Hungarian immigrants. My parents didn't speak very good English. My brother was a manic depressive, and a bit strange too. There was a bit of the Gypsy in us and a lot of the Jew and no high born blood at all, and I just thought her family, your mother's family wouldn't want any part of me or my family. So, right after we fell madly in love in Veracruz and went everywhere holding hands, and so on and so forth, I went back to my room, packed my things and returned to Maryland. I never said a word to her about any of it, and you know, I just broke her heart. And my own at the same time. But I'm telling you the truth: I was afraid."

I have read her letters and his letters, and though she was the artist in the family and so expressive, he, as it turned out, was the better writer. Somehow he got her to understand that he was "not good enough for her" and she forgave him and came to Maryland from New York and they eloped and were married and their wedding announcement said –

> Hear Ye, Hear Ye –
> Married
> Dorothy Little
> Sidney Hausman

And their two names were printed under the word married, and that was that. They had two children, my brother was born in 1942 and I was born in 1945 and our parents were these two love birds all the days of their lives, which were many, as I can attest. And when they died, first my father and then my mother, I scattered their ashes in the lake where they'd started out, and the ashes didn't sink. They sort of swirled around for a little while and then, I swear that this is true, they kind of met and, for a moment or two, the white ash seemed to gather into two shapely forms, whereupon they joined together and sank, slowly and deeply, glimmering all the way to the bottom of the lake.

Open Water Swimming

Open Water Swimming first appeared in my short story collection Castaways: Stories of Survival. *I come by my water experience, naturally and humbly. My father was a distance swimmer and a lifeguard and my mother was a high-diver. I took up free diving, salt water deep diving without a tank, and that became "my sport." I have now spent a half-life deep diving in all kinds of waters and weathers, some dangerous, some calm. Important, to me, is the connection between open water swimming and writing. I discovered writing in swimming. In writing I learned to hold my breath.*

A few years ago, when my wife and I were living in Jamaica, we took a trip up the coast on a whaler. We were between Port Mariah and Port Antonio when a violent storm came up suddenly and threatened to swamp us. One of the passengers in our boat had a bottle in his hand, and when a big wave struck him, the bottle turned into shards. We had never seen waves of such force, worse, we'd never been at their mercy.

Fortunately we got out of that scrape in one piece, but it left a question in our minds—What would we have done if the whaler had overturned in those twelve foot, angry seas? Could we have swum the three and a half miles to shore?

I'd been trained as a Sea Scout when I was growing up and we had been in Jamaica for many years and had experienced all kinds of stormy weather, but the question of survival at sea now began to haunt me, as a man and as a writer. As a certified scuba diver, I knew my capabilities under the sea. But what about on top of it, in storm conditions? Could I handle myself in a riptide? In swells more than twelve feet high?

To answer these questions, I began to swim in the open sea. This is not something I encourage anyone to do who has not had previous experience as a free diver and swimmer. As a trained lifeguard, I knew how to swim well—but I had never really pushed myself to the limit. So now I started swimming by myself along a mile long reef. In the months that followed, I found myself out beyond it, where the depths ranged from 55 to 300 feet, swimming towards an island three miles distant. The round trip from Blue Harbour to Cabarita Island and back, was about four miles total. The current between Little Bay on the reef side and Cabarita on the other, was so strong that no one attempted it. This seemed to be the grandest challenge of all, and once I was in good shape, I went for it.

I found that by alternating swim strokes—sidestroke, backstroke and breaststroke, I could handle long distances without tiring. However, an active player in my workouts was the constant silent partner called Fear. This included predatory fish, barracudas more than sharks, but worse than these stinging jellyfish that could, and sometimes did, paralyze my shoulders—fortunately, just for a short time during which I usually floated on my back.

On one trip I was stalked by a curious or famished barracuda of about five feet in length. He followed me almost to the beach with his toothy under bite and his primal eye always coming closer. (This particular fish was finally caught by a fisherman after attacking a swimmer about a year later.)

Another time in a tropical depression, I found myself caught between a forest of staghorn corals and a battery of coral heads, which left me no choice but to dance on the froth when the tide sucked out, and to sort of surf when it came back in. That was a touchy situation but I managed to get back in with only one gouge on my right ankle.

During a similar predicament, while cruising the coast with mask and fins, I was suddenly sucked into a marine cave. Then I was hurtled through a barnacled tube that spiraled twenty feet or so, and let out in a mysteriously quiet azure cove.

Cramping is probably the solitary swimmer's worst enemy. I learned to give myself calf and leg massages in those rough waters where I was a mile or more from shore. One of the things I did while I swam—to keep my mind entertained—was to work on stories I was writing. Often these tales had to do with mariners who were shipwrecked, and I was able, while swimming, to visualize them completely. Sometimes, I became them; or they became me. Whichever way it was, I was beginning to understand that survival swimming involves so much more than being in good physical shape.

I discovered that it was more mental, perhaps, than physical. This explained why characters that I was writing about began to seem more human in my writing. They got tangled up, for instance in sargassum weed, and imagined they were being pulled apart by a giant squid. Friendly porpoises turned into hungry sharks, and even a tiny swallow of saltwater turned into a life-snuffing tidal wave.

The mind plays all kinds of games with you when the bottom disappears underneath, and there is nothing left but blue, big blue miles of empty sea, where the swimmer feels the myriad eyes of the deep are trained on him. Open sea swimming brings you face to face with the most primal fear there is—staying alive. Sometimes I had to fight back the overwhelming fear of drowning even when I felt okay, but because the shore seemed too far away, and the more I swam towards it, the farther it seemed to recede. Optical illusions and mind games run rampant in deep water, open sea swimming.

Well, eventually, after nine years all told, I had a storehouse of experiences and a lot of words on paper. But I was not writing a book and my writing, like my swimming, seemed more for exercise after a while than for any specific purpose. The truth was, I wanted to write a sea adventure, but I did not know what to write about. I couldn't tell endless tales about swimming the north coast of Jamaica.

Then, one autumn when I was back in the states, a close friend, Jonathan Huntress, sent me two boxes of archival maritime tales from his father's nautical library. Dr. Keith Huntress, Jon's dad, was a well-known author and archivist of shipwrecks and disasters. Some of the books had the scent of Penobscot salt on their yellowed pages. Most were first-person narratives written in the 19th century. With the books came a message from Jon: "My father would've liked knowing that these are now in your possession. Maybe you will be inspired to use them in a book of your own."

These sea stories came at a pivotal time for me. In them I found just what I was looking for—stories of common men and women who were forced to deal with uncommon events in and on the ocean, and also on land. All were castaways, shipwrecked people, who had to learn from scratch what it meant to survive. They seemed to lose all sense of time and place. They fumbled and foundered on islands and keys, and some were driven to insanity.

Interestingly, the tales I read were not unlike some of the ones I invented while I was swimming myself. I felt a great common bond with historical people, who were born in strange times and on faraway lands, and they were, I thought, just like me. They were swimmers in the sea of life, struggling to stay afloat.

However, the ocean itself was the main character. The truth is, human beings have never been more absorbed with the mysterious waters of the world than at the present time. Now more than ever stories that reveal the ocean's hidden fathoms draw our immediate interest. Certainly this is brought on by the fact that the ocean is three-quarters of our earth's surface; and we have never lived in closer proximity to it. Nor has this world of water been tamed or much influenced by human technology or our desire to be one with it.

So we are today not unlike the brave mariners of Homer's time in ancient Greece—still wary, still worried about the next big storm. Rogue waves, tsunamis, hurricanes and all wild weather phenomena are our common lot. Ships like the Titanic are still being built, and still being sunk by the sea. The ocean, above and below the surface, is an unknown frontier. As unfathomable as what we like to call "the vast reaches of outer space." We will probably never conquer the ocean.

In the stories I have chosen to write for this book, you will find identifiable characters from human history. However, as I swam farther and farther from shore--in swimming and writing--I became the people I wrote about.

I was one with the widowed woman who found God in petrel feathers; the marooned sailors who found love and charity on a sun struck sandspit; the man who cruised round the world in a rebuilt boat and who fought pirates and ghosts with his wits; the swimmer who could not drown but could easily die on land; the furious soul who succumbed to madness on an island of beasts; and the seeker of solace on the great river of grass.

All of these I became in the swimming and the writing. And, in the end, I knew there was nothing better in life than keeping the head and the heart up—and when you cannot see the shoreline, always putting one hand, one word, in front of the other.

Gerald Hausman

The Ancient Itch

We live on a barrier island off the mainland of Florida. It's a place where there are no condos and no-see-ums. We like it here. There's plenty to like and plenty not to like but once you get in the island groove you either don't want to come out of it or, for one reason or another, you can't. We have people named Mango Jack, Darryl-with-Teeth and Darryl-with-no-Teeth. There are plain Darryls, too, but we don't count them. People have seen jaguarundis here and eighteen foot saltwater crocodiles and Burmese pythons that share the canals with monitor lizards as large as alligators. (We also have a Win-Dixie Supermarket.) I wrote The Ancient Itch for Gulfshore Life Magazine, and it won an award. I got a lot of calls from toothless and toothful Darryls telling me to pipe down and not write so much. "You'll have people visiting us," they said. "Not as long as we have the ancient itch," I said.

A large green tropical iguana ran across Stringfellow Road yesterday, and I had to stop and look twice to see what it was.

Was it really an iguana?

Or rather, is this Southwest Florida?

The reality is that some of our unspoiled barrier islands (and even the well-combed ones like Gasparilla) are running wild with loopy lizards and other exotic runaway reptiles. We now have boas in the Everglades and monitor lizards that roam the north end of Cape Coral. The sometimes-six-foot monitors get into the mangrove fringes of Pine Island. I saw one the other day and did my usual double take: Was it, is it, where am I?

What author Paul Theroux said while kayaking here applies: "You can travel for days among the low and misleading islands on the outer reaches of Charlotte Harbor and never see a golfer, which I suppose is one definition of wilderness."

Our father-in-law, an avid golfer said, "You have it here, the wilderness. But what are you going to do with it?" I would answer like Carl Sandburg that there is a menagerie, a wilderness inside myself, and this other one outside is a great comfort to me, and I don't always know, or care, the reason why.

Theroux handles his wilderness view with an eye to danger. He paddles innocently and eloquently, as if *imagining* Pine Island rather than *experiencing* it. Meandering in the network of waterways, barrier islands, Indian mounds and reptilian isles, Theroux paints a bas-relief of unmapped subtropical fantasy that is, nonetheless, our reality.

What he's talking about is the watery wilderness that precludes shopping malls, macadam main streets and designer domiciles. When roads of pitch black soften to white shell, when the heart of Florida can be felt within and without, our friend and fiend, the wilderness, is speaking directly to us. Our inner menagerie is under our rib cage, talking.

For some this may happen by merely glancing out a condo window at a panoramic view of the water. For others it may be seeing a footloose iguana, the kind you thought you would see in Ixtapa or Cozumel. Here the creature seems a bit out of context, and yet it is also appealing—to those people that like it. Florida has always had an eccentric wildness about it, a feeling that there are things growing here, even under your own skin, that don't belong. Things that beat to a different drummer, as it were. I call it the ancient itch.

When I first moved here, I had it bad. Well, to be perfectly frank, it sent me—this primordial itchiness—to a dermatologist, who, believe it or not, said I had a case of "bad sand." I could not define that. Neither could my dermatologist. He did say, however, that it was not something you got in Kansas. And he gave me some cream that had cortisone in it.

But my misplaced itch never went away. It's the thing under the skin that makes me love it here. I used to think low tide smelled bad—what did I know, I came from Santa Fe where the tide had gone away a million years before I got there. Now, I take a deep breath of that same mucky elixir and I get the old itch. "You gotta love it," my crab-happy neighbor says, "'cause there ain't nothin' like it." I've heard it put differently. I heard a guy getting off the plane say, "Ahm fixin' t'breathe some air that's thick enough to spread on toast."

"Where you been?" I asked him.

"Up North," he said.

I am called back to my ancient itch whenever I see creatures. Actually, I believe the presence of them, or the lack of them, defines our parameters of primal nature. We need them, not just to instill the ancient itch, but to keep it beyond the instant remedy of cortisone cream.

Alden Pines Golf Course on Pine Island is beautified with homes, but also remarkable animal populations that confound some of our more squeamish visitors. Some there are who don't enjoy seeing an Eastern Diamondback rattler coiled up in a bunker. And there are those who don't appreciate watching a common house cat lifted off its hind feet by a predatory eagle.

A few days ago, a friend invited us over to her house on a private estuary and while we were sipping a little rum on the lanai, a finch flew into the living room. Annoyed that the finch wouldn't leave, our friend began to clap loudly. "What's that for?" I asked. She answered, "I want the bird to fly out of here." I asked where their ladder was, got it, and climbed up to the highest window in the house where the poor finch was fluttering against the glass to escape.

Gerald Hausman

I reached out and the bird was in my palm, its vibrant little body humming with sentient life, droning like a bumblebee with...the electrical impulse of the wilderness. When I set it free by opening my palm I remembered what a friend in Jamaica once told me: "A bird at sea has a wind vibration, a bird on land has a land vibration." This little golden finch still had its wind vibration and I felt it restoring my soul, seeping through my body and enchanting my heart. I felt it humming under my ribcage.

Thankfully, it's still here, the wilderness. Still with us. But can we keep from clapping and trying to make it go away? Can we refrain from trying to clap away the intrinsic, harmless nature that enters our lives? I don't really know. However, I hope we grow more patient; I hope the itch reminds us of who we really are. That we came, as Sandburg says, out of the wilderness, and it is to the wilderness we shall one day return.

I, for one, want the wild nature of the water in me until the day I die. "Life is good," says David Kherdian, "unless you weaken." I don't want to weaken, neither does he. That's why he also quotes his favorite Armenian proverb, "Making a living is like taking food from the tiger's mouth." Every once and a while, no matter what our age or respective financial position, we ought to gamble on a brief tussle in the woods or in the water—with something larger than ourselves.

NOT SINCE MARK TWAIN

I met a 97-year-old named Murph the other day who told me he couldn't swim in the Gulf anymore. Ruddy-faced and winsome, he laughed and added that his girlfriend, the same one who'd restricted his swimming, was twenty years his junior. He winked at me then. "She keeps me on my toes," he said with a quirky smile, "but she's forbidden me to swim with the sharks."

"Are you going to follow her orders?" I asked him. He chuckled, then said, "When I built my house back in the 1940s, A.J. Edwards—yes, the man himself—told me not to invest in Florida real estate because it wouldn't pay off. I just sold my last house for a million dollars, and they had to tear it down because it was old looking and small, and well, if A.J. couldn't drive me off the sand, how's my girlfriend going to drag me off the surf?"

I told him that I used to go for sharky dip off Casey Key in a weird little spot where I always got bumped by some hard, prehensile snouts. "It wasn't sharks, I told him, "but some finny fellows running from them".

"I know exactly where that is," he said. "You get hit by a bunch of mullet making their fast runs to the south. Once I saw something torpedo-shaped, chasing them, and it went right past me. I guess I'm too old and tough to be tasty."

A couple days after talking to Murph, I found myself on Caya Costa. The last thing on my mind that day was a "wilderness reckoning" but it happened, as it often does, when you're not expecting it to.

I was jogging across the width of the island in the late afternoon by myself, when I almost ran into a black feral sow and three little piglets with twitchy tails.

There was barely time for me to throw on my Adida brakes. Grinding to a halt, I stopped just in front of that monstrous, unmoving mama pig. A dark mist of flies swarmed around her head. She grunted. The sweat poured down my neck and trickled into my shorts. My heart was beating loudly.

Funny how things happen. You imagine you're at peace with nature, and then--*bam*—she's right there in your face. And her face doesn't look friendly. It looks truculent.

The first thing you do in such a situation is get calm. And then, if you're me, a whole waterfall of literature flows through your brain while you stand there sweating in the hot sun being examined by two mean little pig eyes in a vast hulk of hair and fat.

But was it so unlike me, who almost ran into it? This grand thing of flank and snout and tusk and hoof?

And thus, I sat down on my own haunches, and took the weight off my mind and my body. The great sow cast a shadow over me and the long afternoon of golden green. I regarded her; she regarded me. Centuries of nut eating, berry nibbling, lizard munching, bird and snake snatching had refined her genetics, and made her grandiose by any scale of the imagination. She was as big as a building.

For a brief moment, I visualized that building hurtling itself towards me and grinding me, mauling me into pulp mash.

All this life-flashing-before-me stuff lasted but seconds, yet seconds are eternities when your life is imagined to be on the line. That huge mama's eyes took me in. I saw her ears flicking, fanning flies. The piglets under her belly squealed; they wanted to move on. But before she did, that giant sow gave my head a brief sniff.

She smelled me. That monstrous-looking beast checked me out, and deciding that I was what she thought I was, she turned and trotted off into the jungled curtains of Caya Costa.

That night I got up from my favorite Pine Island easy chair, and picked up Theroux's *Fresh Air Fiend*. Finding the essay "Trespassing in Florida" I read about how Theroux "...nearly drowned...in one of the sudden storms that frequently explode over these islands." He describes being roughly a mile from dry land when a storm with 60 mph winds nearly outraced him to shore.

What I wanted to know was, how did he feel afterwards? After he made it safely to shore? Theroux doesn't really say. He writes "...the mud flats, the mangroves and the mosquitoes, have in their way kept much of the area liberated, obscure, and somewhat empty..."

There is comfort in those words. For I'd never brag about running into a wild pig that could've rendered me into shreds of red, raw meat. I won't brag on my courage, or for that matter, my timidity, but I will always remember the peculiar, peaceful feeling that came afterward.

I truly felt Theroux's notion of being liberated, obscure, and somewhat empty like the land itself. The sense of knowing that the menagerie under my ribs hadn't *let* me down, but had in fact *sat* me down. The ancient itch was still in me, and it had seen me through another moment of truth. Once again I was one with the wild, the pal of the world, who didn't stick pigs, yet, for better or worse, was stuck to them by the wilderness.

NOT SINCE MARK TWAIN

Out Of This World

Gerald Hausman

A Visit to Cross Creek

This story about Marjorie Kinnan Rawlings was originally published as a poem in an anthology put out by Pearson Educational Publishers. It also came out as a poem in the Longhouse booklet, Bokeelia, *the name of the West Coast town in Florida where I've been living for the past 17 years. I've told this tale at schools because it's a story-of-place and, as we know, certain places have a spiritual power all their own. It's a ghost story of sorts, but mostly it's about being in a haunted wood where you're often looking over your shoulder. And perhaps, Miz Rawlings, as she was called, in a time long gone, is looking over her shoulder as well.*

The orange grove is gone but the silver-board house where Marjorie Rawlings wrote *The Yearling* is still here. So is the hanging moss. I'm a little surprised to see her worktable sitting outside in the sun. I wander in the wet air, swim is more like it. The humus, detritus, tannin-stained tea colored water, the distant smell of decomposition. This could be Florida, circa 1930.

And why would anyone love this place?

So still it seems dead.

I wander across the yard to the orange grove that failed her when it froze. The frost line dropped down the way it does today, the way it did the other day when I came down to see

NOT SINCE MARK TWAIN

Cross Creek. The frost line. There's a town just north of here called Frostproof, and for a reason. It wasn't supposed to come any farther south.

I try to find a single orange tree among the sweet gum and marsh elder and volunteer tropical almond trees soaked in gloom. A fat white possum walks cautiously across the glade that was once spangled with oranges under a winter moon. A small raccoon glides out of a sun shaft and into cool blue, shivery shadow.

The silence grows on me, the sense of being hidden, being bodiless, being A.W.O.L. from myself, my life, from anything human.

I am a shadow shedding shadows. I peel and melt. Walk dainty and glide. Like the possum. Like the raccoon. Like nothing, like nothing at all.

Mrs. Rawlings' woods are wet and I feel I am swimming again. The heat makes my neck prickle. Tribes of mosquitoes sing in my ear.

I come out of the dark into the light. Reborn. There, again, is her worktable shining in the sun, her typewriter -- surprisingly well-oiled -- sits ready for a clack, clack click. I understand why she sought the sun. She loved the rustle of palms of a winter night, the smell of fatwood sticks lighting the grove during one of the not-too-killing frosts.

The little low house, so low and unassuming, is silver-gold this noon that feels like rain. I would like to see the night sky all black and punctuated with white stars. I sit down on her porch, the porch at Cross Creek and sample the syrupy air.

The beauty of being Floridian wasn't lost on this great woman writer who'd fled New York and a failed marriage to wed words, as she might've put it, in a marshy grove sweetened with the fragrance of Confederate jasmine while she wrote about Jody and his fawn and the crippled boy named Fodderwing who was a real kid named Rodney Slater. (I bet there's Slaters on mailboxes to this day.)

"Well, it's all gone now," I hear a tourist tell his wife who holds an old copy of Cross Creek Cookery in her hand.

"What is?" she asks, wrinkling her nose.

"This is," he answers. Beads of sweat sparkle his blue-shaven jaw. "Look at those awful tract houses over there."

I didn't see them, neither did the wife, but now a whole bunch of people are staring with disgust and just like that, like that I tell you, the dream of the warrior woman novelist goes wispy up in smoke and fades, fades away in the clear blue sky.

I look to the grove. The grove that is now gone.

Marjorie Rawlings wrote -- "It was almost worth what it cost me."

What it cost her, in words?

NOT SINCE MARK TWAIN

What it cost her in living every day with poor little Fodderwing and hearing, in her Yankee head, the blast of the gun that brought down the fawn turned yearling, corn eater, crop decimator?

Cost her?

Yes, but a Pulitzer prize came from that writing, those words, this gone grove, this bright table in the sun with the hungry portable typewriter waiting the ghostly fingers to begin tapping again. Machines don't die they just get taken apart by time. They have souls like we do, don't they?

I see a rangy, skinny kid come slowly out of the trees, barefoot and long-striding. No one else seems to see him. Just me. I turn to see what he has, a bobcat skin over one forearm, a rattler skin over the other. The rattler's bronze broad hide is as wide as my waist and I remember my father-in-law saying one swamp rattler he saw was as wide as the shell road he was on.

I stare at the skins -- wanting them, not wanting them. Dreaming there in the sun for a moment, thinking I am back with there with Miz Rawlins, 1933, and a fresh squeezed glass of orange juice in my hand and antses all over the place.

He says hopefully, "You could tack 'em on your wall."

Gerald Hausman

Dead to the World

You get good at seeing ghosts. At first, you just see them. But still you don't really believe them, or rather, believe in them. They say, in Jamaica, "The mind can't see what the heart can't leap" and I accept that as true. My heart learned to leap what my mind couldn't see in Jamaica. During my years there, I learned to see differently. I also learned to write differently. In Jamaica, all storytellers speak from the heart, from the street, from wherever they are -- but from the heart first.

I was lying in a bed on a second floor open window veranda overlooking the sea on the North Coast of Jamaica when I saw my first ghost. She was a little girl with long hair, what people used to call tresses. She was the color blue. Soft blue. A bluish light on boat lost in fog. That kind of blue. Bluey-bluish-nighttime-foggy-blue.

The thing that surprised me was this – I wasn't afraid. No prickly hair. No fright factor. I just lay there in the blue moon that came in through the open Bahama shutter and I felt, well, I felt a little blue. Not so I'd want to cry about it. Not that kind of blue, but when you come face-to-face with a blue ghost, you instantly realize there is such a thing as a spirit world, and that a particle of it is right there in your other-dimensional space.

NOT SINCE MARK TWAIN

One thing about the little girl. . .

When I looked at her to sort of scope her features, she got fainter and fainter.

And disappeared.

Apparently, as I found out, this kind of ghost resisted being studied. You could look but you couldn't stare. And I'd wanted to stare. I wanted to see if I could I identify the color of her eyes – were they blue like the rest of her?

The place where I was staying with my family was an old estate and the caretakers said it was "full a duppy dem." The man's name was Roy. He told me he'd seen his share of duppy. "One time I see a crab--" Roy spoke and when he spoke he made his hand into a land crab crawling on the sand. Roy's eyes got wide. "Crab get big." Roy extended his hand so that it was huge, but the very end-knuckle bent down, crab-like. "Then him tun."

"Him, what?" I asked.

"Tun."

"What's tun mean?"

"Him change-up him shape."

"Oh, I see. Into what?"

"Inna shape of a dahg."

"What kinda dog?"

"Ugly dahg yuh nevah wan fe see, mon."

"Big teeth?"

"Big teet," he answered.

"Red eyes?"

"Yah, mon, red yeye."

"Why is the dog so scary?" I asked. I wasn't really afraid of the dog, more so the crab. Roy's hand-crab was fearsome. But I still wanted to see it again. He wouldn't do the crab, though. Or the dog.

While Roy was talking, he was crushing almonds out of their shell and we were both eating them. Little tiny hermit crabs were popping out of their tiny stolen shells and Roy lined up a dozen or so, and we made bets on which one was going to be the winner. A little bitty baby, beeby, Roy said, won. Beat out all the big fat crabs because, of course, they had heavier shells. Roy said, "A lesson in dat." Same time, on the radio, there came a song called Long Shot about a horse that was running a race and died right before the finish line, and so, got the name Kick-e-Bucket. I felt so sorry for that horse. I still feel sorry for that horse, and for all horses, and crabs and dogs, for that matter.

Roy was pounding almond husks and he said, "Kick-e-bucket go fe heaven, Ger. But crab dem, dog dem – dat two dat I see, dem go noplace. Dem just live like you see dem until the day come when dem dream you and tek your soul wid dem."

"What happens then?"

"Well, dem become you."

NOT SINCE MARK TWAIN

I thought about that for a long time before I fell asleep. I thought the little girl might come back but she didn't. I fell asleep, and woke into a dream. At first I was all air and light and color, a pink streamer flashing through the night. It felt good. I was out of my body into the body, if you'd call it a body, of some animate, unearthly thing. Some alien form of life. If you can imagine the way it looks when Olympians throw that tight-wound crepe into the air as they tumble around, well, that's what I felt like – that paper streamer. But the more I streamed, the lighter I felt. Soon I was invisible – still streaming but with only the slightest of light emanating from me.

I could go anywhere I wanted.

I soared past some ginger lilies and scared the night-drunken bees waddling on the fronds. I zipped by a fruit bat hanging upside down under an eave, a croaker lizard with huge glassy eyes on a porch rail, a crab, a dog . . . Roy sleeping flat out on his back on a cement bench, arms hanging all the way to the ground.

I flashed through an open window leaving a vapor trail of pink dust in my wake.

And there I was. Yes, me. Sleeping like Roy.

I sniffed my way into myself, and I woke with a sniffle. My entire body was glowing, especially all around my chest and heart. I felt wonderful. It was the best feeling I'd ever had. It was – I couldn't describe it if I wanted to. I stayed awake for a long time, waiting for it to happen again. It didn't.

In the morning I told Roy what had happened.

"Dem dream yuh," he said with a smile.

"Who?"

"The spirit dem."

"What kind of spirit?" I asked Roy.

"You don't see it? Good spirit, Ger. Dem was the water moomah what guard the whole water under dis island." He nodded and touched me on the shoulder. "No all de spirit dem bad. Some good. You feel irie?" Irie is the Jamaican word for feeling good, and I felt better than I ever felt in my life and I told Roy that. He laughed. "So you do see it."

"Yes, I said. "So will it happen again?"

Roy said, "Me no know."

It didn't happen again.

Just that once.

But in that once, I felt the potentiality of all things.

I am waiting to be dreamed again. For one of those good entities to breathe me into a dream of its own and take me out of my body for a whirly, swimmy ride in heaven on earth.

And it seemed to me that people who do not fear life should never fear death. I had learned that, even without a body, I was more fully alive than when lying in bed asleep.

NOT SINCE MARK TWAIN

For asleep and undreamed, I was nothing if not dead to the world.

Gerald Hausman

Man Taken Aboard UFO

The story was begun on the Mescalero Apache Indian reservation in Southern New Mexico in the late 1970s. My friend Etienne said there was a bear outside our tent. Was it a bear, or an alien, as he'd first said? A bearlian? Two previous publications of this story -- first in the novel No Witness, *then years later, in the novel* Stargazer. *Twice I added odd facts that came back to me. There won't be a thrice.*

I don't know why I was doing this – camping on the Mescalero Indian Reservation with a guy I barely knew. I guess I thought I was going to get a story out of it. I needed one. Hadn't written anything in years and when Etienne said, "I have a feeling this weekend I will be taken aboard a space craft that comes from a distant planet and …"

This was enough for me. I didn't need to hear the rest – just the idea that Etienne Saronier believed he was The Little Prince, or something.

I don't know how he did it. His whispery French accent, I suppose. When he spoke it sounded like the narration of a journey already begun—and, oh well, so it had.

While we were making a campfire under the ponderosa pines, I listened to him talk. "I have this feeling, you know, that ever since I was a child, that it would happen to me – one day I'd be taken. When I was a little boy living in France, my best friend at that time had a very disturbing dream. He got up from his bed and looked out his window--"

"In the dream he did this?" I asked.

"Not in the dream. He had just had the disturbing dream. Now he is at the window looking out."

"Got it," I said. But I wondered what the dream was. Etienne went on.

"So my best friend looks out of that window, and what does he see?"

"I have no idea."

"He sees a flying saucer, all silver and bright, sitting in his father's cow pasture. And who do you think is standing in the open hatch door of the saucer?"

I shook my head, shrugged.

"My friend was astonished."

"Who was it then?"

Etienne touched his thumb to his chest. "Me! My friend could not believe his eyes because it was me inside there, with the doorway open, and waving at him. And here is the funny part – I am also lying asleep in the bed opposite my friend."

"You were spending the night?" I asked.

"Sleep-over sort of thing, you call it. Yes, me asleep in the other bed. And me waving from the portal of the saucer."

Then, for a little while, Etienne busied himself with helping me make supper over the fire. It was dark by then and the fire was cheery. Soon we had some tomato soup starting to bubble and the wind came up and crept around the camp and I remembered that we were on Apache land.

"Look, quickly – there!"

I turned my head in the direction Etienne pointed towards. Just in time to see a little scribble of light that streaked downward from the night sky and ended up somewhere on the desert floor some sixty miles away from our campsite. White Sands Missile Base was down there and, no doubt, there were things we didn't know about their little missions with satellites.

"What was that?" I said, "satellite?"

Etienne gave me a dreamy lemur stare. "Maybe we will be taken together," he said, casually stirring the soup with a fat spoon. We slurped in silence. The temperature dropped. It was autumn in the high country. The wind got more playful and threatened to toss our tent down into the desert. I pounded some extra stakes in the loopholes, and nailed the little cocoon tight to the earth. Then I got my down jacket; Etienne was already wearing his. We went from soup to hot chocolate. Etienne's eyes never left the heavens.

Out of the dark, he whispered just over the wind. "I can sense danger. You know that I can."

That gave me a creepy feeling. "Why do you tell me that?"

"I am picking up your fear," Etienne said. He drained the last of the cocoa in his cup. He was still staring at the sky. The fire was down low, just red coals which the wind would breathe upon and turn a ripe orange. From where I sat on a round stone, Etienne looked like a sprite, an elf. Even his ears, large and lemur-like, looked odd in the dimming afterglow of the fire.

I said nothing in return to Etienne's offbeat comment about my fearfulness. But I had to chuckle because he was right, I was feeling weird, to say the least. But not much worse than that. Just weird. I looked into the space of sky between the pines. There was a round hole full of stars, and I gazed in that direction.

As if Etienne had commanded it to happen, there appeared a steadily moving, lightly glowing object, like a kind of uncertain star. It moved in an arc and began its descent along the curvature of space. "What is that?" I said aloud.

"Satellite," Etienne said, then: "Why don't you admit you're afraid?"

"Because I'm not." Saying that unnerved me.

I glanced at my watch. The luminous dial said it was 11:13. The wind picked up and growled around the tent. "If it makes you happier, I'm scared," I said. To no one, as it turned out. Etienne had risen without a sound and was peeing on a pine tree. He was a ways off and couldn't hear anything I said with the wind moaning.

I unzipped the cozy nylon tent and slipped into my cozier down bag, but it had gotten so chilly, I kept my sweater on. Etienne appeared seconds after I nestled in, and got into his sleeping bag. "I heard that," he said.

But he didn't say what.

I was so tired from the long day's drive from Santa Fe to White Sands and then to Mescalero that I found myself almost laughing myself to sleep. What was I nervous about anyway? Etienne was crazy. Big deal. Who isn't? So I had no story. Big deal. I was safe and snug. I loved camping and this was camping. And Etienne, well, he was a friend just the same. Crazy or not. I slept, and dreamed. And saw a little boy standing in the portal of a flying saucer and he was waving to me, and it was Etienne. I woke with a start.

I looked at my watch. It was twenty-six past three. I was hot, sweaty. Unzipping my bag, I let the cold, crisp mountain air circulate on my fully clothed body.

My heart gave a shudder. I lay there, feeling the rush of fear fly from my adrenal glands and take further flight through my bloodstream. I was wide awake. And frightened. There were two unison breathings. One came from Etienne. The other came outside the tent. Two distinct bodies of breath.

Within and without. I listened. Could the thing outside the tent hear my heart thunder?

My mind was working hard to reason it out. The sound of breathing inside was obviously Etienne. But what was the breathing outside the tent? My mind deserted me. Deer, bear, elk, coyote?

I sucked up my own breath, and held it, so there was no distraction.

Listening, I heard two things. Etienne with his deep intake, followed by a rattle-snore as he let go of his breath. Or as his breath let go of him.

Outside the tent – same exact thing. It was as if there were two Etienne's, one within, one without. I placed my index finger over the entrance of my right ear. The outside breathing stopped. The inside continued drawing and rattling. I released my finger and the outside breathing resumed.

At that moment it would've been a relief if the exterior sound had moved. If it had proven itself to be that of an animal. Even a bear would be a relief. As it was, my fractured mind was forced to accept a single conclusion – Etienne had a doppleganger and that double being, so to say, was right outside, waiting for one of us to do something. I lay and sweated it out for quite some time. Maybe an hour. Then, all at once, I unzipped the tent flap, and rolled out into the starry night. For a moment I sat in starlight, breathing deeply of the pine-scented air. Then I poked my head back into the tent. Etienne was sawing logs, in out, in, out.

    I chuckled. There is such a thing, I reassured myself.

    It's an auditory illusion, I told myself.

    And got back into the tent, soft as a mouse, so as to not waken the stranger in the dark.

    I got comfortable. Glancing at my watch, I was surprised to see it was almost five AM. I'd wasted a perfectly good night's sleep over – what? Nonsense. Scaredy cat nonsense.

    The last thing I remember seeing before sunrise was Etienne floating in a dense blue, incandescent fog a couple feet off the tent floor.

NOT SINCE MARK TWAIN

Talking Adobe

Talking Adobe was published in New Mexico Magazine in 1993. But long before I wrote it, I heard it. The teller was Baldamar Coca, who also speaks on my audio book Stargazer. *Baldamar called his story The Talking House and he said it was well-known among Taosenos. I built --with my cousin Peter and my brother Sid -- our adobe house in Tesuque, and on one of our forays we met an old adobe-maker who put parts of his children's discarded toys in his mud when he made adobe bricks. His stories were like that, too -- made of mud and sand and the echoes of children's voices. The walls only talk if you listen. But if you listen, the walls don't always talk.*

Spanish legend holds that the devil dwells in the mountains of northern New Mexico. This is because the mountains running south along the spine of the Rockies were called by the Conquistadors, Sangre de Cristo, Blood of Christ. Which, evidently, is where El Diablo, the host of darkness, likes to dwell: within the dark heart of the mountains of Christ's blood.

So goes the mystic legend.

Andrew was thinking about this one day, driving on the Dulce road down to Taos when he spied an old man with a crooked back and staff. He was not exactly hitchhiking, but he leaned out into the road as if to lure a ride.

His ploy, if such, worked.

Andrew stopped. And gave him a ride all the way to Taos Pueblo. They went along a secondary dirt road, and Andrew brought him right to his door, for which he thanked him by asking Andrew into his house to have a bowl of chili.

He was a banged-up old outskirt Indian, living in the willows that grew around the river. His face, rugged and Plains-cast, suggested that this northernmost Pueblo had intermarried with the people of the prairie, farther to the south.

A mile down the road the Pueblo raised itself out of the rosy glow of late afternoon, thin streams of smoke rising from the adobe chimneys. Inside the old man's house, it was dark, musty smelling, a peppery taint of chili and wood smoke engraved in the mud-plastered walls.

As soon as they got inside, the old man went around, as if blind, feeling the walls with his hands.

"What are you doing?" Andrew asked.

"Seeing if the walls have anything to tell me," he replied. He placed his head against one of the walls, listening and smiling.

"They do," he said.

Andrew considered his comment the eccentricity of a strange old man, and left it at that. The old man busied himself then with starting a fire in his woodstove, and heating up the chili he'd made the day before.

NOT SINCE MARK TWAIN

Presently, from within the old iron stove there was born the heartbeat of heat, the expansion of iron, the prattle of pine consumed in flame. Andrew noticed that the old man wore a pair of beaded deerskin moccasins.

"Some people say it isn't possible," he said, stirring the chili with a wooden salad spoon. He laughed to himself, not to Andrew; then, looking up, he added: "They say that walls can't talk."

"My experience," Andrew said, thinking of his many adventures with Johnny Thunder, "tell me that all things can, and often will, talk--but we have to listen."

"Ahh," said the old man appreciatively. He raised his chin and brought it down several times. "That is the problem with the world," he said sadly.

Then, after a while, he remarked: "You can, if you like, put your ear to my talking adobe."

Andrew gave him a quizzical glance.

"Do not be too surprised what you hear," the old man said jokingly.

He paused in his stirring to see how this was taken.

Andrew gave him a nod, a smile, and pulling his chair near the wall, leaned over.

And listened.

There was an immediate stirring that came to his ear. It sounded like bumblebees, buried somewhere in the wall. He listened a little longer, and the humming changed.

Gerald Hausman

And it seemed to him there were the rudiments of linguistic sounds in there, far off utterances of Tanoan tongues. The bumblebees joined, mating in the cores of the mud walls.

And then again it sounded like the underlayment of woven voices you sometimes hear on a wintry night when the telephone line is being battered by snow; not white noise, in this case, but rather, its opposite--red noise, old, old Indian talk.

Andrew remained, ear to adobe, until the old man called him to the table to eat. He left the wall puzzled, wondering what it could be, as the rational mind tried to get control of the intuitive heart.

"So, now you know," he said, handing Andrew a clay pottery bowl of steaming chili. He seemed very proud of the wall, pleased that the right person had listened to it; and that, now, along with himself (and who knows how many others) the talking adobe had spoken.

And then, while they ate, he told Andrew a story.

"It is all magic earth," he said, "all of it. You see, long ago, before the Pueblo was here, some Indians were camped over there under the mountains. These were my ancestors. One day they saw a man ride out of the pine forest on a white horse. He was tall, well over six foot. He had a beard, yellow in color; his skin was white and he had clear eyes, the color of the sky.

"Now this man rode right up to my ancestors and he said that he had come a long distance, and would they be so kind as to share some of their food with him. This they did. After he had eaten with them, my ancestors asked the man how far he had come. He told them that he had come from a distant star. Pointing at the heavens, he showed the great distance he had come.

"My ancestors then asked him why he had come to their land. The man looked surprised. 'Do you not know?' he said. They shook their heads, for they did not. 'I have come to help you make a settlement on your land,' he said. And he went on to say that what he wanted to do was help them make a very large and very tall lodge that all of their people could live in together. He said he knew how to do this, and that he was sent by the Sun Father to help them accomplish it."

The old man paused in his narrative and got up to make some coffee on the stove, which he fed some more pinon logs. Andrew waited and when he returned he told me the rest of the story.

The chili was hot and burned Andrew's mouth. The coffee was hotter and burned his mouth again. However, each, as well as the old man's story, warmed Andrew's heart.

Shortly, he went on to say that the strange white man, the visitor from a distant star, showed his ancestors how to build Taos Pueblo.

"That is why," he said, "the Pueblo is so tall. And it is the reason why it resembles the buildings on the old island of New York. It is," he laughed slyly, "our own little skyscraper."

"Did the man with the beard stay with your ancestors?" Andrew wondered.

He shook his head, sipped his coffee, frowning.

"He left."

"But did he ever come back?"

The old man seemed reluctant to say more.

"Who can say?" He shrugged. "The whole thing's just a story."

"Some story."

"Yes," the old man repeated, "it is some story."

It appeared that he wanted to say a little more, but that he was not certain that he should, or would. He paused, pursed his lips.

"Our windows," he said, "face the direction the man went when he rode away and returned to his star. And our earthen walls still speak the way he spoke so long ago. His story is in our walls."

"I see," Andrew said. But he did not; not fully.

"Yes," the old man added gently, knowing that Andrew did not understand. For understanding does not come with hearing, but through listening with the heart.

They then sat in polite silence.

After a while, Andrew got to his feet and thanked his host.

The old man followed Andrew to his car.

Andrew slid into the front seat.

The old man said, by way of leaving: "One day he will return."

"Why will he do that?" Andrew asked.

The old man looked to the north where the fir trees quilled the mountains.

"One day he will return to finish the Pueblo."

It was almost dark, the pumpkin afterglow lingered on the woolen hills in back of the five-story prehistoric structure known as Taos Pueblo, the oldest, continually occupied home in the old New World.

The farthest mountains were russet in the last light of day; beyond them the great sleeping mountains, whitened with snow, and now, at sunset, blood red in sun-glow.

"Who was the man?" Andrew asked.

The old man chuckled, his eyes shining. This was the thing he had wanted to say, and now he could say it, for it had been asked of him.

"They call him" he said deeply, "Jesus on Horseback."

Gerald Hausman

Let's Not Tell Anyone About This

This is one of those is-it-true-tales. Unpublished and untold, I'd completely forgotten about the old flying chair until my cousin Kyle told me about it the other day. Then I remembered, and wrote it down.

My cousin Kyle said to me, "Do you remember the little room on the third floor of Granddad's lodge overlooking the lake?"

"I remember it --not much bigger than a closet. There were two pieces of furniture -- a marble table and an old rotten, horsehair chair."

Kyle said, "When we were five we'd go into that secret room when no one was looking."

"It was at night," I echoed.

"Our parents thought we were fast asleep." Kyle laughed, a little hysterically, I thought, but, yeah, it was kind of funny the idea that we were together in the shadow room with the big gloomy chair.

"Mmm," Kyle purred, "the big chair was our secret sharer. Remember?"

"It's coming to me -- something weird about that," I admitted. "Did the chair have . . . powers?"

NOT SINCE MARK TWAIN

It was coming back faster than I could think. The narrow steep stairs winding up to the third floor. The creaky door to the secret room. The knotty-pine nearness of the walls. The absence of air. The dust. The forbidden secretness. The horsehair smell. The moon on a thousand year old, threadbare oriental carpet.

There was the old chair, so vast and solid, a kind of personage that beckoned children to sit on it. Yes, it had powers, all right.

We crept up to the chair and inched our way up onto the sprung horsehair cushion. The chair smelled ratty and rotten. The room so airless and close, as if whatever lived within the walls needed every bit of oxygen that was available, and none left for a couple of errant and disobedient kids.

It was clear to me why the chair was so special.

The chair transported us to places we didn't want to go.

Settled into its cavernous shell, the chair somehow blasted off like a rocket, flew us out of the Lodge and skimmed us across the lake.

Not only that, it skimmed us under the lake. Then it soared us into the clouds, and above the clouds, took us into outer space, sent us galumphing into the Milky Way where we tailed the tails of comets.

And then, always and forever buried in my memory, the old chair turned around and brought us home.

Gerald Hausman

We'd blink -- and be in that stuffy, small, airtight empire of dust.

I remember that, one night, Kyle met me in the darkened hall in front of the secret room, and she whispered, "Tonight we're going to do something different."

"What will it be?"

"I'll show you." Kyle was mysterious and mischievous. Sometimes I forgot she was my cousin. For she was more a magical, dream friend.

Soon we were seated, elbow to elbow, in the chair.

I remember how the chair was woven of twigs, millions of strands of twigs and it was, in reality, a once upon a time tree that was now a square, squat painted tree that looked like a chair and had horsehair cushions, bottom and back.

We sat together, Kyle and I, and the chair rocked out of the secret room and into the open night of sundry stars.

All was well until Kyle hissed -- "Let go of the chair!"

I would not -- but she did.

And went spiraling into space.

Tumbling into eternity, she spun away from me while I gripped the fat arms of the chair until, at last, the chair upended me.

And there I was -- tumbling the heavens with Kyle.

Flying.

There was the white noise of moonlight.

NOT SINCE MARK TWAIN

We were not flying so much as we were flight.

The thought of flight.

And always, at the end of the ride, the old trustworthy chair scooped us up and brought back to the airless attic room.

"We mustn't tell anyone about this," Kyle warned. She was younger than I but so much wiser. I wanted to tell the world; sadly, I agreed not to tell.

However, the weird thing is, as soon as we left the room, we forgot about the chair. We forgot about flying. We forgot about the thought of flight. In time, we even forgot ourselves, or perhaps the idea of ourselves as cousins with a magical chair.

Some time passed. Granddad lost almost all his money -- or so we were told by our parents. The great Lodge was sold for petty cash.

The horsehair chair went with the Lodge.

Nor did we think of the strangeness of this. The Lodge where we'd grown up -- gone. Not occupied by us, inhabited by . . . strangers.

More time passed. We grew up. We forgot.

On all, some sixty years went by in a twinkling.

Kyle and I became grandparents.

A few months ago, we were sitting, Kyle and I, on the dock by the lake below the hill where the Lodge had once been (it burned to the ground in 1976) -- and an eerie wind came out of nowhere.

Kyle's beach chair, and mine, didn't move because we sat hard upon them, waiting for the wind to blow by.

And it did, finally. But it soon returned and pushed both of us into the lake.

Kyle laughed, and said, "Can you hold your breath like you used to?"

"I think so."

Kyle said, "Let's find the chair!"

I said, "What chair?" but she didn't hear me.

I followed her underwater. The lake was as clear as air.

We swam around and held our breath for what seemed many minutes at a time. We saw seaweed, beer cans, stones, bluegills, sunnies, bass, pickerel and pebbles of all kinds.

We surfaced and breathed. "The chair!" Kyle cried, treading water and looking down.

She dived.

I followed.

Kyle pointed at something dark and gray with her finger.

In the amber glitter of the spring fed lake, the hunkered shape resembled an immense mossy stone.

There it was -- our old friend, the horsehair chair.

Kyle and I were flying overtop, looking down.

First she, and then I, touched the twiggy, woven arm, then the sprung matting of the cushion . . . and, then, it happened all over again.

NOT SINCE MARK TWAIN

We sat in it --

-- and flew across sunlit coves and sullen caves.

And the chair rocked the rookeries of the swamp, scattering turtles and herons, and ferrying us far and wide across the lake where the water was dark and green and deep and there we abandoned our bones and entered the preternatural realm of pure chairless flight, the thought of flight, holding on to nothing but our breath which never diminished, for like a fish we breathed without knowing it.

When, at last the chair brought us home, we watched it bubble down out of sight. We climbed on the dock, our fingers pulpy and white.

I started talking about the underwater ride.

But Kyle put a finger to her lips, whispering, "Let's not tell anyone about this."

And I haven't until . . .

just now.

Gerald Hausman

To the Blue Mountains of Jamaica

Roger Zelazny, science fiction master, was not only a friend -- but, when we wrote the novel Wilderness *together, he became my best friend. This story is based on some of our conversations together as well as a dream in which the things I describe here happened the way I have written them. Roger always wanted to go to Jamaica with my wife Lorry and me. In my dream and in this story, he did just that.*

In my most recent dream of Roger, he stands before his home in Santa Fe, an adobe house at the top of a steep rise that looks out on the Sangre de Cristo mountains.

Not surprisingly, Roger doesn't talk about himself; he talks about his children.

"How do you like Trent's story?" he asks me.

"It has the iron stamp of success."

"From the old forge." He chuckles, looks slantwise at the sun.

I see that Roger seems to be busy doing something. Then he turns back into the shadow of his adobe castle, which is, itself, overshadowed by a blue-green, serpentine mountain.

"There are some people waiting for me."

NOT SINCE MARK TWAIN

The mountain stirs, blurs, time ripples across its infinite sinews. It slides off into the void, and is gone. Roger is gone, too. I waken. Wondering, as ever, why I cannot stay and talk more with this friend of mine, this man who is so deeply wedded to my unconscious, my spirit mind, my writer's heart.

Once, more than ten years ago when Roger was still on this earthly plane he told me, "I believe in the bardo, that sequestered zone of death-in-life where a man, having just passed, may ready himself, through thought and divination, for the next experience."

I am surprised when he speaks of this because we are not talking about the Egyptian *Book of the Dead* or even his version of it, *Creatures of Light and Darkness*.

"How long does the bardo last? What length of time?" I ask.

Roger pauses for a moment, then says, "Of that I'm not certain. Might be it's different for each person."

I see Roger quite often now. He is the same as he was in life. I am the one who is different, I suppose. Last night I saw him writing, typing the way he always did with his portable manual typewriter on his lap, his concentration greater than my ability to summon him. I stand and watch him type.

They make music, a stream of changeless poetry that flows out of the throat of a nightingale. It's a symphony, not meant to be read, but to be heard, and I hear it well, and am lifted aloft by it.

I wake, still dreaming. My eyes open. It is only later—fully awake—that I realize Roger has just taught me something about writing; that it is not a conversation between two people, the author and the reader, but it is a symphonic outpouring, a silver rain of divine mind.

Once, in, let us call it "real life", Roger and I rained words on a page together. We stormed and spat forth forks of lightning. But there was a bardo-like time of waiting, of meditation before we worked together. It happened like this:

One day I told Roger the tale of two mountain men, John Colter and Hugh Glass. Colter was chased by Blackfeet Indians for 150 miles in the area in and around what was later named Yellowstone National Park. Hugh Glass, eviscerated by a bear, was buried alive by friends who thought he was dead. Glass dug himself out of the dirt and crawled one hundred miles on his belly over the Grand Valley to the Missouri River.

Roger liked the idea of the story—the runner and the crawler. But he told me we had to wait a year before he had time to tackle it. That year lengthened into two. And thus I learned the most important lesson there is: waiting with grace. Or, if not grace, at least not angst. Roger told me, "To wait is also to write. We'll get to it. Sooner or later."

It was what I most feared. The later.

NOT SINCE MARK TWAIN

Roger knew it, too. He let me live with it.

When it did come time to do ColterGlass (as we called it then—later it became Wilderness) Roger was eager to begin, not that he had the time to do so, but his willingness surprised me.

At that time, he was writing two other novels, plus a variety of short stories and essays, all in good style and, of course, good humor. I wondered how he could accomplish so many things seemingly at the same time.

Roger, the juggler. The wondrous mage who never dropped anything on the ground. Keeping it all in the air, the days and nights floated over him, and he played, he danced, he joyed over the words he wrote, or rather the words that came joyously out of him. If it was work of the bodily kind, sitting and typing for long hours, he never complained of it. He seemed at ease with everything he wrote, and it was all as real and as spontaneous as his speech.

Our shared novel, *Wilderness*, was a lesson in how to write without pressure. How to let the characters be who they are, not who you want them to be.

Colter, the runner.

Glass, the crawler.

"At some point," Roger said, "the roles may change. The two men reversing their positions in life."

"Historically, though, they didn't change," I told him.

Roger smiled. "Shall the runner slow down, and crawl? And the crawler, one day, will he get up and run?"

"What will that do to the story?"

"If it happens, and I'm not saying it will, but if it does it will make an unreal tale seem more real."

A little later on, when our collaboration was almost at an end, I told Roger that I couldn't conclude a certain chapter—didn't know how to stop the pell-mell action.

"I'll see what I can do," he said.

The following day Roger gave me an envelope.

My ending was the same. He hadn't done a thing to it.

But the next chapter was his. It was three words long: "The hawk soared."

I told Roger, "Well, that takes care of Colter. Now what about Glass?"

A couple of days later, he showed me the Glass chapter, which was ten words long: "And growling, the bear raised himself onto his hind legs."

"I guess that solves it, " I said.

"Don't be afraid to let the unexpected pop up," he said.

To this day, those are my two favorite chapters in the novel.

There are many things Roger taught me. But, towards the end of his life, we shared, not writing, but being. I was going

NOT SINCE MARK TWAIN

to Jamaica a lot in those days and Roger said that he was really intrigued with the Blue Mountains that rise from sea level to seven thousand feet, and where, in the tropics you can sometimes have a flurry of snow at the summit.

Roger asked, "What is it like up there?"

Having just returned from a Blue Mountain trip, I spoke rhapsodically, "The coffee trees spread out in the lower elevations, the cheese berries litter the paths above the Jacob's Ladder, which is cut in clay straight up to the plateau that straightens into a primeval forest of ancient cycads, and this plateau is followed by air plants and orchids galore, and then come the stunted trees near the top and the tall windswept grass at the very summit from which you can see all the way down to Kingston. I was afraid I'd get blown off the mountain."

"Take me there sometime," he suggested.

I promised I would do that.

It has been many years since I made that promise, and only last night did I try to fulfill it.

In the dream, I am waiting for him on top of Blue Mountain Peak.

Roger comes along, flying.

"A new chapter," he says, opening himself on the wind and blowing right past me.

Gerald Hausman

Pirate Breath

As luck would have it, I wrote a small short story collection one year while we were living in Jamaica. The collection is called Duppy Talk. *Duppies are Jamaican ghosts and my experience with them is in the book but also in the History Channel program* Haunted Caribbean. *We recreated the essence of Pirate Breath for them and I acted out my own part with my wife, Lorry. We had fun filming this, but it didn't end there, as you shall see in this story.*

I breathed pirate breath, once.

I was in Jamaica staying in the old estate of Noel Coward on the north coast. One night I fell asleep listening to the cheep and chime of the tree frogs and when I awoke there was a pirate sitting on my chest.

He wore a piratical red felt greatcoat with gold filigree. His shirt was loose and open, and soiled. He stank to high heaven. There was every smell you might imagine on this stinking man. He carried a fragrance of forlorn sweat, fetid animals, swilled rum, tobacco flakes (his beard full of them) bad teeth, oaken casks, sour smoke and other less nasty odors like cloves, which he apparently was chewing to sweeten the smell of his dead gray teeth and to ease the sting of his mouth sores.

NOT SINCE MARK TWAIN

I bore the man's weight on my chest until I could stand his smell no more. In point of fact, he weighed nothing, nothing at all. And when I kicked him off me, he went like a featherweight into the air, landing hard on his brass-buckled shoes.

The pirate drew his sword and I prepared myself for his next attack. But as he raised the curved blade over my head, he, or rather his image, dissolved before me.

All that was left of him was his piratical smell. I awakened my wife Lorry, and said – "Bloody pirate's been sitting on my chest!"

Half-asleep, she mumbled, "I smell him. Where is he?" She was sitting up, peering. There was the sound of the sea shuffling around the coral heads. The tropical night was clear, tree frogs piping, croaker lizards *critching*.

"Where is the pirate?" Lorry asked with a yawn.

"He left."

"Out the door?"

"He disappeared."

Lorry smiled, murmured, "Ghosts."

Not me. I stayed awake all night.

Just before dawn, I heard the ring of a pickaxe, the chink of a shovel. Then silence. The last croaker lizard barked and then the pocket parrots owned the jeweled, Jamaican morning.

My pirate visit seemed to vaporize in the Saint Mary sunlight. Fishermen sang on the reef as they dropped their fish traps into the turquoise bay. It was a beautiful, friendly day and came to a quiet and peaceful end with another lovely evening, slow and somnolent and seeping darkness from Firefly Mountain that loomed over the old estate. Going to bed, I remembered the pirate had tried to cut off my head with his sword. The old sword was red with rust rather than blood. And, as the man faded before my eyes, his clothes, his sword, his face all turned to rags and ruin, sinew and bone. After this uncanny exposure, he vanished.

Let me point out, I am not afraid of ghosts.

In fact, I like them.

Even the sword-raising kind.

Yet this unknown, ancient man meant to murder me – why?

The color and sound of the day had drowned out all else, but now, as I slipped into bed, I wondered what the pirate was after, and why me.

I swung out of bed, put on my shorts, went downstairs and spoke to my friend Roy.

Roy was meditating under the guava tree by the bamboo fence. He smiled when I told him about the pirate. "I think him look fe something dat once belong to him. Where your bed is, Ger, dat where him bury, dat where him dig."

"Did he see me then?"

"Him dream you."

"His dream being his dead life?"

Roy chuckled. "Him no dead. Him trod de world just as before."

That fact, if fact it was, made me feel much better – about the pirate. At least he had something to do. A job of work.

But it didn't explain why he wanted to chop me with his cutlass.

Roy explained that by saying, "You inna his way. Inna him dream."

Six months later, when I returned to Jamaica, I was with a camera crew and a producer and director from the History Channel.

They liked my Jamaican ghost story collection, *Duppy Talk*, and had asked me to be an advisor on the shoot.

One story, which I'd discussed with them, was the midnight encounter with the pirate.

The first morning of the shoot, the director, Jim, said, "You know, I like to do these stories of hauntings, and their relationship to human history, but I don't feel them in my bones the way you do as a writer, or participant."

I laughed and said, "In Jamaica, they say 'who feels it knows it.'"

"Isn't that a Bob Marley lyric?"

"Yes."

"Well," I suppose I don't feel it," Jim told me with an amiable shrug.

The producer, Alyce, made fun of Jim. "I'm a bit more open than you are," she admitted. "I've never actually seen the stuff we re-create for History Channel, not like you have, Gerry. But tell me, off the record, did you really, truly see that pirate? Or were you dreaming about him?"

I wanted to explain how they dream us, not the other way around, but instead I said, "I saw him and I smelled him. My eyes were wide open."

"What did he smell like?"

"Black tobacco, golden rum, shit and gravy."

"Ah-ha," Alyce said, "That's rich."

Jim just stared at me.

We finished the rough footage of the film in five days and on the fifth night Alyce excused herself right after dinner, saying she had to pack and get some rest because the crew was heading out in the morning to do some more ghost stories in Puerto Rico.

At breakfast the following morning, Alyce came downstairs from the upper veranda of Villa Grande. She did not look well. Despite having a bit of a tan, her face was pale. Her hands were shaky at the table. I asked, "How are you doing, Alyce?"

"Not so good," she confided.

"What was the matter?"

NOT SINCE MARK TWAIN

"I thought it was a joke, at first. That big sleigh bed upstairs -- it started bumping up and down. I thought it was Jim, playing a trick on me. Then — she shook her head – "Whatever it was, demon or joker, it actually kicked me out of bed. I landed hard on the cedar floor – Bam. It was all over after that. I stayed awake the rest of the night, like you did after you saw the pirate. The whole time, my mind's turning it over. Still haven't got hold of it yet. My first real ghost encounter. Feels pretty weird . . . and goofy, at the same time."

"They dream you," I said softly, but I didn't go into it, and Alyce didn't ask.

"I don't ever want to get slammed on the deck like that again." Alyce got up and said she had some more packing to do, and that was the last I saw of her. Jim thought it was all very amusing. Said it might've been an earthquake. You get them here, don't you?"

"We get them, but there wasn't one last night. We would've felt it. The whole little coastline quivers and shakes. Things fall off the walls."

"Yeah, things like Alyce," Jim joked. "She'll be all right, though, don't worry about her."

I didn't. But I knew what she was going through. When I looked into the graveyard eyes of my pirate, and saw that he was alive, it was a moment I'll always remember. His smell hung in the air like . . . well, like the grave.

Gerald Hausman

In coming days Jim edited the film so it would appear the following fall on History Channel, and I helped edit the script that went with it, and we exchanged emails for a while. He was back in Los Angeles and I was in Florida. Then one day, I got one of the strangest emails ever.

Dear Gerry,

I don't want to make this more awkward than it is. You know how skeptical I am about this supernatural stuff. I've heard all of the writers talk about hauntings, and I've managed to stay objective about it. Makes my job as director and editor a lot easier. Well, this is what happened the other night. After I put the film to bed with some last minute cuts and edits, I put myself to bed. My son sleeps in the next room and both of us went out like a light. Middle of the night, the bed starts shaking. I was sure it was an earthquake, we get a lot them in L.A. But the house is still and silent and no objects are moving. Just the bed. Finally, whatever it is kicks me off the bed onto the floor, and then in my son's room, I hear the same thing at the same time -- a crash – and my son yells, "Hey, Dad what's happening?" Do you think Henry Morgan could've followed us back to Hollywood? What does he want -- his own film? He better get a ghost writer. In all seriousness, this crazy thing really happened just like it did with Alyce. I'm wondering about a lot of things lately.

Best,

Tim

NOT SINCE MARK TWAIN

Moments Of Truth

Gerald Hausman

Snail

This story happened before the turn of the last century in the Canyon Creek country of Montana. I first learned of the mountain man Liver-Eating Johnston from Dr. Raymond Bunker when I was living in New Mexico in the 1960s. Bunker was a legitimate story link to the character of Johnston whom he had written about and also to the story of Plenty Coups, the wise Crow chief who, if he did not change history directly, offered another version of it in this story. This originally appeared in the book Horses of Myth by my wife Lorry and me.

One hundred years ago there was a horse named Snail, a sleepy, sulky, and generally lazy mustang. Not that there was anything wrong with that, really, but in the little corner of big Montana where Snail lived, horses were prized for their ability to look nice and to race well.

All that was lost on poor Snail.

Oh, he had the noble Barb and the blooded Arabian in his ancestry, but so well hidden. Somehow, the sloping rump and convex head, the pretty, wide-set eyes, small muzzle and pointed ears were buried in hard-caked dirt, which was just one of the reasons he got the name Snail.

NOT SINCE MARK TWAIN

You see, he liked to roll when it rained; and he liked to dust himself when it didn't. It didn't matter how often he was curried, for he had a longing for the creek bottom and its sticky, slicky Montana mud.

Snail was mostly mustang, as far as pedigree goes, but, at a distance, all muddy and spattered and gone-to-seed, he seemed nothing more than a leaf brown horse with a few, true Appaloosa spots on his hind quarters.

There was nothing that stood out about Snail except that he lived up to his name—he didn't move a muscle except to munch prairie grass or take a roll in the creek bottom.

Well, he did have one peculiarity. Snail, like his namesake, enjoyed a bit of cabbage now and again. Snail's owner, Uncle Bill Wooten, who was a pioneer in the area, discovered this one day when he was carrying a ball of cabbage under his arm. He'd just come from his garden and was passing Snail when the darn fool horse took off after him.

Snail was thirty yards off when Uncle Bill noticed that he was about to get run over. Not knowing what else to do, Uncle Bill threw the cabbage head in the air and headed straight for his cabin alongside Sourdough Creek. When he looked back a moment later, Snail was happily crunching down the cabbage.

"Well, well," said Uncle Bill, amused. "Snail found something in this topsy-turvy world worth running for—and, if I do say so myself, what a run!"

The next thing Bill did was call some of his friends. He asked Doc Allen, Jeremiah Johnson (the famous mountain man), and Tom McGirl to have a look at his silly, little mustang, the one everyone thought was a useless pony. They came over the very next day.

Snail, for his part, paid no attention to the men gathered around him. Ignoring everyone, he went on with his munching and crunching.

"Well, what's so special about this not-so-special horse of yours," queried Doc Allen. The others nodded. They had seen all they wanted to see of Snail.

Uncle Bill explained, "Remember how you fellows wanted to find a racehorse that could beat Plenty Coups' famous buckskin mare?"

Jeremiah Johnson guffawed so loudly a raven coughed in a nearby tree.

"You're not gonna tell me that this here hoss of yours can run, are you, Bill?"

Uncle Bill looked slyly at his friends.

Jeremiah picked up a little clod of earth. Uncle Bill undid Snail's tether and held his halter for a moment, while Jeremiah sent the clod of dirt flying like a bee. It nipped Snail in the flank, and old Snail—or young Snail—shivered and wiggled his hind end ever so slightly, and went back to grazing buffalo grass. The incident had passed without his knowing it.

NOT SINCE MARK TWAIN

"All right," said Tom McGirl, pushing back his Stetson "What kind of a trick you think you're pulling, Uncle Bill?"

"Yeah," said Jeremiah. "What'd you get us over here for?"

"Time to 'fess up, Wooten," added Doc Allen.

Uncle Bill grinned like a fox. Then he dipped his hand into his feed bag and produced a big, round, green head of cabbage.

"Okey-dokey, Doc, you hold Snail's halter, but you better let go kind of quick-like when I git to that big fallen tree over yonder."

Off went Uncle Bill, striding like a fireman on the way to a burning schoolhouse. When he got to the fallen log, he called out, "Here, Snail, come to Uncle Bill!"

Then he brandished the cabbage.

At once, Snail kicked up his heels. Then his hooves pummeled the earth, and he took off like lightning. He made it across the pasture before Uncle Bill could lower his hand. In fact, Snail stole the cabbage right out of the air—because Uncle Bill tossed it for fear of being trampled to death.

When Snail was finished chomping and the men were finished staring in amazement, Uncle Bill asked them, "Think we can get ten to one?"

"I think we might git a hunnerd to one," Jeremiah stated.

"Them's odds I like," said Tom with a smile.

"Are you thinking what I'm thinking?" asked Uncle Bill.

Doc Allen rubbed his chin thoughtfully. "I'd say it's time I mosey over to the Crow Indian camp and have a little talk with Plenty Coups. He thinks his buckskin can beat anything on four legs, and there's no reason to disabuse him of that notion."

"We've had…how many races against that buckskin?" Jeremiah asked.

"I'd say, ten for a guess," Doc answered, "and we lost all of 'em."

"That buckskin's got spunk and fire for blood," said Tom.

"But Snail'll take her in a stretch…long as I have a cabbage head in my hand," Uncle Bill added.

So Doc Allen drove his buggy over to Plenty Coups' camp, and he asked his old friend straight-away if he wanted to run his mare in another race. It never occurred to Doc he'd say no.

But he did.

"To win is good," said Plenty Coups. "To *always* win is bad."

"Well, the way I figure it," said Doc, "to always think your gonna win is bad. To *sometimes* think your gonna lose is good."

"What makes you believe there's a horse in the territory that can challenge my buckskin?"

NOT SINCE MARK TWAIN

"Doesn't matter what the horseflesh is, as long as we have our annual get-together. You know, every year when the leaves turn gold, we have a horse race. It's sorta traditional."

Plenty Coups grinned. He knew tradition.

"All right," he said, "one more race. But after this..."

He didn't finish. He just looked off towards the Pryor Mountains and smiled, as if he were planning a trip there soon.

"You mean," asked Doc in surprise, "that this'll be the last horse race?"

And Plenty Coups nodded.

Well, the day of the race came around as quick as the first Montana frost. In other words, it was right there before you knew it. Sourdough Creek was jam-packed with people—settlers and cowboys on one side of the road, and the whole Crow nation on the other.

Plenty Coups came in on a white horse, but his son Ironeyes rode the great and gorgeous tan mare that everybody called Buckskin. Her color was soft as sand and brown as dirt. Plenty Coups let everyone admire her, too—her shining muscled coat, her sidestepping, softly neighing, prancing-hoofed beauty. All the Indians sighed when they saw her dance up a little dust. Then they laughed, when they saw what the settlers and cowboys and miners and trappers were going to run against her—pathetic little Snail!

Poor, pitiful Snail had rolled in some mud that morning, and Uncle Bill had left the splotches sticking to his hair. Indecorous little nag that he was, Snail never looked up. Just kept filling his craw while the Crows circulated around him, chuckling and laughing and making fun.

Plenty Coups shook his head. "This is worse," he said to Ironeyes, "than last time."

Ironeyes smoothed the eagle feathers that were braided into Buckskin's mane, and he stroked her lovely white-streaked nose.

"I wonder why they like to lose so much," he said.

"Because it makes them happy to see us win," Plenty Coups answered. "Anyway, we shall never know what strange things lie in the hearts of these people. They are as much a mystery to us as we are to them."

No one urged the Crows to place their bets. They did so willingly, even wildly. They dropped down treasure after treasure on the big blanket where the bets were laid. There were pelts and plews and beaded belts and moccasins of all shapes and sizes.

To the Crows the race was already won, a mere formality awaited the dividing of the gifts. Their eyes were fixed on the goods laid out by Uncle Bill and the others: bags of flour, coffee beans, rock candy, ax heads, mirrors, beads, nails, cottons and flannels.

Then the oldest wife of Plenty Coups came forward. She carried a huge white grizzly-bear skin, which she let drop upon the betting blanket like an armful of snow. All eyes—both white and Indian—were on that pretty bearskin.

Doc Allen smiled. Not to be outdone, he dropped a brand new Pendleton blanket and a Remington saddle rifle on top of the white grizzly fur.

Next, the horses were led to the starting rope. Snail trudging, as if to his death. Buckskin prancing, as if he might dance up to the sun. While the two lined up, Uncle Bill Wooten felt inside of his coonskin, which was laid across his arm. Then he walked down to the end of the track, and waited for the race to begin.

Plenty Coups took his place beside him.

Buckskin was reined to the starting rope by Ironeyes.

Snail was walked up by the son of the owner of the Sourdough Trading Post, a light-boned youth that everybody called Wee Willy. Now, Willy *was* small. But he was also the best rider in the territory.

Anyway, there they were, ready to ride the race of their lives—if, of course, the horses were willing. Well, one of them was...at least that was the way it looked.

Plenty Coups peered into Uncle Bill's coonskin cap.

"What do you call that?" he asked.

"Medicine," replied Uncle Bill. "What do you call *that*?"

Plenty Coups held up a string with some pale fur on it.

"This is the white tip of the silver fox tail."

Uncle Bill asked, "You think that thing'll win the race?"

Plenty Coups chuckled. "It won't hurt. Do you think your vegetable can defeat my fox tail?"

"It won't hurt," Uncle Bill replied.

Then the two of them smiled at each other, right up until the moment the rope was dropped and the gun was fired, and the race began.

Uncle Bill held up his cabbage, so Snail could see it.

Plenty Coups waved his fox tail tip.

All eyes were on that little sleepy eyed Snail because, although he was behind by a length, he was catching up.

Then, they were neck in neck.

Buckskin, that magnificent sun-dancing mare, edged up by a head.

Uncle Bill thrust out his head of cabbage.

Plenty Coups swung his foxtail string in a circle, singing softly under his breath. The settlers screamed and the Indians wailed, and the two horses drummed the earth so loudly the golden leaves on the cottonwoods floated off their branches and rained down on everyone's head.

And the horses came on with a rumble that made the earth tremble.

Their feet were striking now in timed precision. Buckskin snorting, Snail blowing froth. Both galloping for all they were worth. And then the mud-spotted, begrimed little Snail inched up.

"By golly, that queery-eyed little Snail's gointer win!" cried a prospector.

"No chance," said a tall, blanketed Crow.

They were almost at the finish line when Buckskin came up ahead of Snail once again. On came Snail—the cabbage well in view. And, then, well, that little nose length of his might've won the race...

It just might've.

But who could really tell?

You see, the race all happened so fast. And then the strangest thing of all occurred.

A dust devil rose up off the plains. It spun a tower of white. It billowed up and dropped down; and it settled on the crowd and blinded them.

Now when the dust cloud cleared, the people were fighting over who was the winner—Buckskin or Snail. The people were divided on two sides of the road. They were shaking fists at one another, and it looked as if a real battle was going to break out on Sourdough Creek.

Amidst the dust and confusion, barking dogs, crying children, nickering horses, angry oaths and victory whoops, the people fell back into their separate camps to decide what to do.

"Did you see the winner?" Doc Allen asked Uncle Bill.

Uncle Bill said, "I saw it as a tie."

"They were neck and neck—'til that dust-devil smoked us out," said Tom McGirl.

Doc Allen added, "Snail had Buckskin by a nose, as I see it or, or saw it, or the way it *seemed* to have happened. How about you Jeremiah, what'd you see?"

Jeremiah looked a long way off into the smoky plains, and beyond them, to the far blue mountains. Then he surveyed the two warring camps of angry men and women alongside Sourdough Creek. If something wasn't decided soon, he just knew the racetrack was going to turn into a battlefield.

He ran his hands through his whitish brown, shoulder-length hair, and shook it out. It amused him to see that everyone was equally covered with alkali dust. Even little Snail and broad-chested Buckskin had gone from gray to white and from brown to white. But, as to the race's outcome, he was as stumped as the rest, and he said, "Hells bells, if I know."

Plenty Coups showed up then, his face white as snow. "Who do you make the winner to be?" he asked Uncle Bill, who screwed up his face and smacked his lips and replied, "One or t'other, I suppose."

Then Plenty Coups grinned. "I thought Snail was a loser. But now I know different. Snail is a Thunder Horse."

Uncle Bill brightened, "So you have him as the winner?"

Plenty Coups answered, " I have him as a Thunder Horse."

Jeremiah, edging in, asked, "So you think Buckskin's the winner?"

"I think it shall soon be decided," Plenty Coups said, his grin all gone.

"I certainly hope so," Doc Allen interjected. "Whoever wins is going to be rich as Caesar."

"Was he a great horse racer?" Plenty Coups asked.

"No," said Tom McGirl, "but he was a pretty fair gambler."

"I see," said Plenty Coups.

Then the five of them stood and looked at the treasure that was heaped up on the blanket, piled three feet high—the furs and hides, the jewelry, the store goods and foodstuff.

Pitted against this was the crowd of cowboys and miners and trappers all arguing and shaking fists at the Crows, who were making hostile gestures. Any minute, a bloody fight was going to break out.

It was at this moment that Plenty Coups stood between the two groups and raised his hand. It took a little while for things to get quiet, but they finally did. Then the only sound was the snorting of the two racehorses and the cry of the magpies in the golden cottonwood trees.

Plenty Coups began by saying, "Listen with your hearts, all of you." His sharp eyes found every face in the two crowds. The people grew even quieter, so that the breathing of the horses was all that could be heard. Lazily the wind raised some more of the white talcum dust and dropped some more leaves of sun-minted gold. But no one said a word.

Plenty Coups spoke again.

"We are all," he explained, "as the Great Mystery made us, men and women, horses and dogs, birds and leaves, and grass and dust. These fine things spread out on the blanket mean little to us, those of us who have the life given to us by the Great Mystery. That life I speak of is all that there is, and all that there will be in this time. So, I say now, take these things, these bits of silver and gold, and keep them. This is my decision, and I have spoken."

"Who...who shall take them?" Uncle Bill asked.

Plenty Coups answered, "Let those who have no dust on their face take away the winner's blanket and all that lies upon it."

Now, the people hearing this looked from one to the other and all around, and up and down. But, of course, there was no such person unmet by dust. Each and all were dusted up and dusted down. And all were equals under the sun, including the two horses, who still pranced about the creek with their riders trying to rein them in.

"Is there no winner then?" asked Uncle Bill to Plenty Coups, who answered, "We are all winners and losers from the day we are born." The big grin was back on his face as he finished, "We are winners coming in, we are losers going out. In between, we are glad to be alive." He made a motion for his people to pack up and leave, which they did, but no one made a move to collect the glitter on the blanket that lay in the sun.

"Well, sir," said Doc Allen, as he saw the cowboys lead off their horses and wagons, and the miners tramp back to the hills, and the trappers follow them on their soft moccasin feet. After a short while Sourdough Creek looked the way it always did, and the cottonwoods shivered and dropped fine coins on the blanket that lay in the September sun.

It was time to say something, but the four friends who had wound up the race didn't know what to say. They stood in the desolation of the road and looked at Snail. He looked the same--except a lot whiter--still munching grass and paying no attention to the men.

Uncle Bill still had some cabbage leaves. He let them fall, one by one, and the wind took them to the four corners of the plains. The four friends watched the leaves blow away, but Snail never saw them. And the treasures on the winner's blanket stayed untouched, until the first snows covered them that winter.

Gerald Hausman

And they are there, today, one hundred and ten snows later.

The name of the village that grew up along Sourdough Creek is called Snail's Pace, and it's still is a one-horse town, so they say.

NOT SINCE MARK TWAIN

Curandero

To be blessed by the healing touch is a thing that can't be described in words, and yet, in some ways, this story is all about words. Inexpressible words. Isn't that why we tell, why we write? To express that which cannot be said, cannot be written. In doing so, we find in ourselves the gift given to others -- the healing touch. The missing syllable that heals the hurt heart. Or perhaps relieves the stress in the lower back. I have told, but never written this story. I feel lighter for it.

I was doing this thing called the kip.

You're flat on your back with your hands behind your head, and you snap up into a standing position. In my teens and twenties I could do this in my sleep. But in my forties it got harder and I got more brittle. One day while I was teaching my students the kip, my back went out and refused to come in.

The class finished with me lying in the grass saying ta-ta to my students. They left the field and I lay there wondering how I was going to get up on my feet. Or worse – if I was going to get up at all. My lower back just wasn't there anymore.

Somehow, by miracle of mystic navigation, I slithered to the top of the hill, climbed into my old Volvo and somehow managed to drive myself to Dr. Santiago Aguilar's studio off St Michael's Drive.

When you hobble into Santiago's healing sanctuary, there is a sign over the door that says, "You are blessed coming in." Above the inner lintel it says, "You are blessed going out."

I managed to get myself into the little room and Santiago who is blind stood in the space before me, and smiled. He could not see with his eyes. But with his heart, his hands and his mind he could see perfectly. He had only to be in your presence to know who you were and why you'd come. "The old kip, eh?"

"Yeah," I said, "did it again, I'm afraid."

"How many times have I told you you're not an eighth grader any more." Santiago chuckled, then, "Okay, get up on the table."

I lay flat, face down, while he ran his fingers along the knobby vertebrae that I call my backbone. "It's not down here," he whispered.

"It's in my lower back," I told him. "Feels like broken glass."

"It feels like it's *there*," he commented. "But actually, it's up *here*-- and his fingers went up to my neck, and down a little, and paused. "Here," he said softly. "What'd you do, put an apple in there?"

"What do you mean?"

"Feel for yourself," he said. I heard his quiet feet moving away and then coming back. I reached up and touched the first vertebrae, or perhaps the last, of my spine. Santiago was right – big as an apple.

What would happen next I knew.

Splash of ice cold alcohol, then his kinetic fingers going after the apple, then his familiar, often repeated note of caution -- "Look out, hombre, here she comes!"

Whammo.

Lights out, lights on, lights out.

All kinds of little lights in a variety of orbiting colors, and then --pain gone silence. After which Santiago's warm, affectionate, triumphant laughter, "Got it!"

Happy to be free of pain, I sat up quickly and said, "Santiago, I feel like I know you."

"You *do* know me."

"I mean, I feel I know you better than I *seem* to know you. That make sense to you?"

"I make you feel better? You like feeling better, so you know me really well." He chuckled softly, sighed.

I pressed him a bit more. "Would you tell me something about yourself? Maybe our paths crossed somewhere or other --"

" -- Maybe, hombre. You ever live in Las Vegas?"

"New Mexico or Nevada?"

"The second one isn't real," he said. "First one, now, that exists big time, for me."

"I used to live there," I told him.

"You ever attend Highlands University?"

"I did."

"What years?"

"I was there from sixty-five to sixty-eight."

"Maybe we saw each other," he said.

"Were you . . . *sighted* at that time?"

Santiago laughed. "I've always been sighted, hombre. But I was blind then, as now. Did you take Chemistry with Dr. Amai?"

"I did indeed."

"You remember the guy who blew up the lab?"

"How could anyone forget that?"

"That was *me*," he whispered.

"What?"

He laughed roughly, and loudly, for him, letting me know that it was all right to be surprised, astonished, or whatever I was feeling, and then he said, philosophically, "It was a good thing that happened, hombre."

"How can you say that?"

"Well," he replied slowly, "first off, nobody got hurt. Second, I realized – when the explosion happened – that I was a blind man who had no business being in a laboratory full of chemicals."

"What did you do after the blast? How did you get out of there?"

"The way I got out of everything. I walked. Wasn't hurt at all. Nothing broken but test tubes, pieces of wall and ceiling. Walked away like nothing happened. Went all the way to the Spic and Span Bakery. Found an alleyway back there and lived in an abandoned shack that was used by winos who slept off their bad nights during the day. I couldn't see them but I sure as hell could smell 'em."

I gazed at Santiago. The more I looked at him, the better I seemed to remember him. "Did you go to the bakery to eat?"

He snorted, chuckled. "I ate like a dog in the alley. The winos couldn't see very well themselves, so they thought I was one of them. They always had some food they'd been given by Mrs. C. de Baca who owned the bakery. You remember her?"

"She had very large . . ."

"—Napoleons," he finished. "I lived on them. Day old, two day old, sometimes three-day-old. I ate them with relish."

"You liked them *that* much?"

"No, I didn't like them but the old winos said when you put relish on them you can cure a hangover."

"Did that work?"

"I don't know. I never had a hangover."

"So what happened to you?"

"I went home to my grandmother in Villanueva."

"Villanueva? That's far from Vegas."

"I walked."

"How?"

"By walking."

"You're lucky you didn't get hit by a car."

I felt a warm hand touch my neck. His fingers had a tingly touch. Every time he touched me, you felt the tiny electrical crackle of Santiago's powerful magic. He was from a long line of New Mexico mystics, herbalists, curanderos, people of power.

"The apple isn't there any more," he said, adding wryly – remember, no more kips!"

"No more kips," I agreed.

I got up from the massage table and paid him twenty-five dollars, which was his charge for any amount of healing with his hands. Even if it took all day, his fee was still twenty-five dollars.

As I walked under the lintel, I read the sign – "You are blessed going out."

I was walking as easily as I had ever walked in my life. It felt good to be afoot, to be upright, to be moving swiftly in the light of day, having ears to hear and eyes to see, and I felt the sudden rush of unexpected, grateful tears that ran down my face.

NOT SINCE MARK TWAIN

"I remember you now," Santiago said as I got into my car.

Gerald Hausman

The Greatest Novelist to Come out of Cuba

Writers come in all kinds of packages. This package said, Do Not Open. But I opened it anyway. I do not regret it. How else are you going to find out what writers think of their own work? One thing I have noticed about writers, in general. They are all a bit lost. A bit out of -- and yet deeply stuck -- in their heads. Present company excepted of course.

I was a guest storyteller at the Miami Book Fair for over ten years. Every year I looked forward to seeing some of my favorite authors come and go on their way to panels or meetings. Elie Wiesel came into the bar one time with a distracted head of gray hair and a cigar. He was looking for someone. I gazed at him and he thought I was his appointment, and then he smiled realizing his error and I smiled, and he left. I still remember the warmth of his gaze, the beautiful distraction – not just the hair but the whole man -- and the aroma of his expensive cigar.

Another time I was in the author's lounge known as the Hospitality Suite. The gracious hostess, Juanita, who knew me from years of visitations said, "See that man over there? That's the greatest author to come out of Cuba. He's internationally known and admired. I think you should get to know him."

"What's his name?" I asked.

She pursed her lips, wrinkled her nose and said – "I forget his name but he's very famous, and you'll know him the moment you talk to him. He's in the program, here."

Juanita handed me a Miami International Book Fair Program. I searched through it while she took care of some authors who'd lost their way, but I couldn't find the Cuban master's photograph in the magazine.

The author was sitting and looking quite famous by the vast picture window that was a picturesque Key Biscayne skyline and seascape, so lovely in the early morning sun it was easy to imagine you were on a movie set.

On impulse, I sat down at the author's table, and introduced myself. I don't know what possessed me -- but without any hesitation, and as if I'd known him all my life, I asked this perfect stranger what he was writing.

That broke the ice. He roared with laughter and said, "What am I writing? What am I writing?" He looked at his companion, an attractive woman, sitting beside him. She shrugged, said sarcastically, "I don't know what you're writing."

"It's just a question," I said, grinning.

"—And a very good one," he replied earnestly, face full of intent. You see," he continued, "it's . . . ah, well . . . complicated." He extracted the word *complicated* slowly and with great emphasis, drawing it out as if he were smoking a Cohiba and blowing soft, thick blue smoke into the air between us.

He then frowned at me, brow deeply furrowed. There were beads of perspiration on his forehead and even though the AC was frosty, he was wet with sweat.

With a beautiful oratorical flourish, he commented -- "You have asked a very deep question, my friend." The voice was rich, heavily accented.

"What am I writing?" he asked the space between us. But then, dramatically, he gazed into my eyes, patted the table with his broad hand. "It's the future," he said, smiling provocatively.

There was a moment of silence and he laughed, shook his head, looked at me again -- "It's the past," he murmured.

"The past *and* the future," I added politely.

He brightened. "It's science fiction . . . it's history. . . it's interesting."

I nodded.

Then his animated face fell. "I'm afraid it's really just boring," he confessed, "b-o-r-i-n-g."

"You can say that again," his female companion said with a sigh.

"I'm sorry," I said sadly.

"Don't be," he said, smiling. "It's interesting."

"--Oh?"

"You see, the truth is, it's one thing, and then it's another." He fired a look across the table at his lady friend. "In truth, it's all things."

He looked thoughtful, then depressed. He laughed.

I sat waiting. I knew there was more.

At last, he clapped his hands together. "Look," he said, it's nothing." He said this cheerfully. His face darkened. "Yet it *is* something!"

My escort arrived, I excused myself, but as I stood up, the Cuban novelist grabbed my hand. "You ask such a deep question," he confided, "but the point is, I wrote it, I'm writing it, I will continue to write it -- all you have to do is read it."

I promised him that I would – the moment I find out who you are, I told myself.

At the end of the day I went to the front desk of Hilton to ask for an extra copy of the Book Fair magazine with all the pictures of the authors so I could find out who he was. I planned to buy his book and read it that same night.

The girl behind the desk asked me who I was. I showed her my author's badge, and she said admiringly, "Michael Hausman. You're the director, aren't you?"

"No," I said apologetically, "I'm the storyteller."

"Of course you are, Michael, I know your films."

"You have a better memory than I do."

Gerald Hausman

My badge really did say Michael instead of Gerald. And I suppose his said Gerald, but at least Hausman was spelled right, and all the kids liked my stories and I sold a lot of books and it really doesn't matter who you are as long as you know what you're doing. (I must make a note of that.)

Tyger, Tyger

This one originally appeared in the anthology Wheel of Fortune *edited by Roger Zelazny. I'd been having a hard time explaining to Roger how William Saroyan had influenced me as a young writer, and here came an opportunity to explain it in story form. I used a mix of fact, fantasy with a generous sprinkle of Saroyan's manic optimism; I also used some characters of his -- the lucky little mouse, the gambler writer, and the man named Doughbelly. All in all, I feel it came out right. Roger got it anyway.*

New York City, 1939

One week of gambling had turned my fancy to mice, or mouse, I should say. There was the Mouse, the one and only, the great genius, the luck-bringing mouse of The Great Northern Hotel.

Yes, the Mouse...

He, or it, arrived one night while I was unable to sleep. That whole day I was down at the waterfront, across from Pier 17, playing floating crap games with the longshoremen, who, during their lunch break went behind the empty boxcars, or behind the piles of lumber on the docks, and gambled away their weekly fortunes. The sun was out, but so was the wind, I got pretty cold, so I bought myself some scalding coffee.

I was having a hard time with the Play, which wouldn't get itself written without a little personal wager. So I bet myself that I could write all three acts in less than two weeks. Hence, the gambling and the mouse...but now I'm getting ahead of myself.

I'd made a friend of the great black crapshooter and game manager, Doughbelly. He would always call the points of the game in a funny way, throwing his big deep bass voice like that other "belly," the twelve-string bluesman, Leadbelly, from New Iberia, Louisiana. Every time my friend, Doughbelly, saw that I was down on my luck--my gambling luck was no better than my writing luck these days--he slipped me a ten, so I could get back into the game.

So went the days. The nights fared no better. Until the arrival of the Mouse. When he came along, like a midnight muse, everything changed. He came prancing into my life the night I'd lost everything, including fifty bucks I borrowed from Doughbelly, and now feared I couldn't pay back.

I was sitting on the chair in front of the desk where my Corona was perched, feeling as morose as seventy out of work violinists, when along came the Mouse with his mouth stuffed full of greenbacks.

NOT SINCE MARK TWAIN

I blinked a couple of times. The Mouse looked for all the world like a miniature retriever. So help me, he had five ten dollar bills pressed between his little mouse-white teeth.

Now I knew I had the shakes, and I knew my head wasn't screwed on right, but no matter....

The Mouse didn't seem to care if I were a desperate author down on his luck. He just stepped up and dropped the bills at my feet.

There I was, shaking like a leaf in a ragtime wind, staring insanely at those crisp, new-minted bills. Those fivers were so fine, and the Mouse holding them delicately, so his teeth wouldn't mark them. And then he just dropped them at my feet, and I picked them up, and realized the time had come to throw the shakes.

"Could you do that again?" I asked the Mouse.

The Mouse said, "Sure."

"How about a carafe of hot coffee and some poppy seed rolls?"

The Mouse looked dubious about that, but he nodded and high-tailed it out of the room. I took a hot shower, and shaved for the first time in three days.

Afterwards, placing the clean stack of bills beside my typewriter, I began to write. Thunder is more like it, I began to thunder, because when I get going, the portable Corona starts gyrating like a belly dancer, making one hell of a racket.

In a short while, room service knocked on the door. A young man in a red uniform with shiny buttons and gold brocade, offered me a tray with a carafe of fresh coffee, and some hot croissants. I slipped him a ten, but he refused it, saying, "It's on the house."

Then he winked, knowingly, and apologized for not having any poppy seed rolls.

I tossed down ten cups of coffee, one right after the other; and I ate a prodigious number of rolls. Then, back to the Corona, the momentous thunder, the powerful punch of words on paper, the miraculous creation of a play, a play, a play!

At dawn, I awoke, my head cradled on top of the Corona. I'd fallen asleep, typing. The last word, before I hit the deck, was "sayeetyujkfogl." Or something to that effect.

Anyway, I roused myself, took another scalding shower, came out of the bathroom. There was the Mouse, back again with another stack of bills, clean and crisp as the last batch, only these were tens.

"Where do you get these things?" I asked the Mouse, as I rubbed my wet hair with a dry towel.

He said, "I steal it, of course."

"All right," I sighed, "that's your business, not mine. I'm not here to improve your morals, any more than you're here to improve mine. Besides, the play's the thing; and the thing's coming along fine. Time for some relief--a little refreshment out there in the big world."

I folded the new bills, stuck them in my pocket, and left the Mouse to his own devices. First thing, I paid back old Doughbelly. Boy, you should have seen him laugh, which explains how he got that name. His big round belly shook like a bakery sitting on top of the San Francisco Earthquake.

Doughbelly told me to take my place, but I told him that today wasn't my day to shoot craps. Then I headed out to the track.

On the way, I stopped in at a little bar that I like to frequent, a place called Number One Opera Alley. There I met a man whose father had been stomped to death by a circus elephant. This gentleman--and I use the term loosely because he was a loose gentleman--was furiously poring over a copy of *The Racing Form*.

"Seabird," the bleary fellow suggested--no, insisted.

"Why?" I asked.

"Because I like the sound of the name."

"That's no reason," I crabbed.

You see, I happened to know that Seabird was a worthless piece of horse poop ever since she crashed the barrier two years ago. Names, of course, have little to do with winning, but that got me to thinking about the Mouse, and I touched those brand new bills that were now burning a hole in my pocket.

Well, there I went -- straight to the to the track to bet on that worthless scamp, Seabird!

Why?

Because I liked the sound of the name.

I was cautious, though. I put a half dollar on her across the board, dollar and a half in all, four bits to win, four bits to place, and four bits to show. And Seabird, the windy steed from the salty south, came in first in a nine horse race. Suddenly, I had a bunch of money.

Now, if I'd wanted to, I could have bought a new suit of clothes, gotten a pair of decent shoes, ordered a hot meal at the Algonquin. I could have gone to Canarsie, or Hoboken, or Patagonia. I could have flitted off to any city in the world, and I could have lived it up for a while, until the money ran out, anyway. But why press my luck?

What I did, I went back to Number One Opera Alley, and gave half my winnings to the man whose father had been stomped to death by a circus elephant, my Seabird informant. And, I want to tell you, that felt just wonderful.

The look in that guy's eyes when I handed him the dough carried me far into the night. I wrote page after page of the Play, worked myself deep into Act Two.

The stuff was good, possibly great. Somehow, I knew this was the big one. But that night, the Mouse didn't return. I kept looking over my shoulder, but, alas, no Mouse.

No matter, I had still had the good feeling inside me.

If the Mouse didn't show, so be it.

One page or so before dawn, when I was almost done with Act Two, I got myself in a jam. Or, to put it another way, my characters got fed up with the author, and went on strike. I had no idea where to go because they weren't about to go with me. If I couldn't keep my characters on their feet through Act Two, how was I going to get them all the way to Act Three?

I went to the window and watched the sun come up. Lighting a cigarette, I inhaled deeply, drew the smoke all the way down to my toes, and thought a little bit about my life. Thus far, all things considered, I'd been pretty lucky. Though the critics might not agree, or the head-shrinkers, I knew I had my fair share of lucky days.

To begin at the beginning: I was always a gambler. My first book came about because of a bet I made with myself. I swore that if I could not achieve some amount fame in two months time, I'd quit writing, and take up a useful profession like optometry or plumbing.

So, every day thereafter, I wrote one short story. One story a day for two months, non-stop.

What were the odds?

Fame in two months, or quit.

Million to one, right?

Gerald Hausman

I sent my daily output, every day, to one magazine editor. Don't ask me why. It seemed like a good thing to do at the time. He happened to be the best editor of the best literary monthly on big American market. So I wrote him one letter, just one, and said: "I am sending you one short story each day in the hope that you will find my writing acceptable for your magazine."

Somehow, that comical threat, combined with the evident talent of those early stories, charmed the editor, who not only published a half dozen of them, but got them into the most prestigious short story anthology in the country.

After that I wrote one collection of short stories, every year for the next ten years, and all of them sold voluminously, making me one of the best known writers of short stories in the world.

My next bet with myself was that I would write a screenplay, on order, for the movie mogul, Louis B. Mayer, who was the hottest producer of big shot films in Hollywood. I bet myself that I could achieve this in less than two weeks time.

I appeared at MGM on a Monday, Corona in hand, and before the day was out, I'd pitched a story to L.B., and he'd pitched me back a six figure advance. Then I sat down and wrote a heartfelt fable about the life and times of a Western Union messenger boy. This was a safe story with a happy ending, with a song or two thrown in that you could whistle to, and L.B. lit up a large Havana when he read it. But before the cigar was half done, the fat little man was weeping.

After that, I was no longer a contract writer for MGM, but the hit writer of a hit film that was earning me more than two hundred and fifty thousand dollars, the first time around. The second time around, I turned the script into a novel which went Book of the Month, and became a national bestseller that netted me another quarter of a million.

However, my next wager with myself was to triple the money I'd earned in Hollywood, and do it quick as a wink. So I gave myself ten days, and wound up at the track where I met another one of those mysterious strangers who put his finger on the well-penciled program, and said: "If you want my advice, put all your dough on Dixie Girl."

"Dixie Girl," I said, "are you sure?"

He drilled me with his eye.

"Sure I'm sure," he said.

Somehow, that haunted shadowman with the piratical eye seemed to be another of those oracles of the moment, and I took his words as pure gospel, and put three-quarters of a million dollars on Dixie Girl.

Then, I sat down and awaited the outcome.

At the far turn Dixie Girl began to run over the other horses; she began to eat them up. She was out in front by at least six lengths. I figured the next thing that was going to happen was a chorus of angels singing Hallelujah over my head. For I believed, right then, that I was the champion writer-gambler of the whole world.

And then...

Some mechanism in the great void went awry.

Dixie Girl, the winningest horse that ever was, tripped and fell, shattered her right foreleg.

That was the end of that poor inglorious horse; as well as the end of me, the luckless writer-gambler, who was now all but broke.

In fact, I was right back where I started--only worse. My luck was gone. I soon discovered that I could no longer write, and though L.B. still believed in me, and offered me a shoebox office at a hireling's wage, nothing came of it. I was shot dead with that poor horse, Dixie Girl. As she went down, so did my fortune, self-esteem, and writing talent.

For the next ten years, I lived in grubby hotels, and made a helter-skelter living any way I could. I traveled around a lot. Whenever possible, I gambled, for I was given to gambling; and gambling, sad to say, was given to me. However, the losses were no longer large. They were as thin as my output as a writer, which is to say, non-existent.

Enter the Mouse.

Enter the Play.

Enter two acts, save two pages, of the best writing I have ever done.

Exit the Mouse.

And there I was, staring wearily at the rose-tinted dawn, wondering what was next, when...

--Enter the Tiger.

He padded up to me, looked balefully into my eyes, and whispered, "Lune."

The Tiger was orange and black, the latter color laid out in perfect stripes of infinite harmony. And with that one word, "lune," the Tiger cancelled the despair of the moment.

"I don't get it. Don't you speak English, like the Mouse?"

The Tiger said, "Purr."

Its enormous tigery eyes were the color of the golden dawn.

"Purr," it repeated.

"Oh, well," I said."

"Purrrrrr," it replied.

Then it struck me that the Tiger was talking Tiger.

"Are you a friend of the Mouse?" I asked.

The Tiger said, "Purrrrrrrrr."

For quite some time, the tiger and I looked at one another. Then, slow-blink, it looked away, perhaps at a painting on the wall; maybe, though, at nothing, because tigers are fond of looking at nothing, and then pretending that nothing is something.

It occurred to me in a flash that with the advent of the Mouse, I had achieved hope. However, with the entrance of the tiger, I had something greater than hope. What I had now was faith.

Yes, with the entrance of the Tiger, faith.

I sat down at the small desk in room 125, on the fifth floor of The Great Northern Hotel in the great city of New York, and my fingers were poised expectantly over the keys. Then, as I began to make thunder, I saw the Tiger lie down, and begin to purr.

I stopped thundering.

The Tiger stopped purring.

I tapped a key, making the letter 'T'.

The Tiger rumbled an incomplete purr, which rattled, and stopped.

Then I knew what the Tiger was, and I began to thunder again, to draw order out of chaos, to bring light into the dark, to make precise that which was imprecise, to glorify the absurd, and make ridiculous the sanctified.

And the more I pounded those keys, the louder the Tiger purred, so that it sounded as if I were typing in a garage with an idling diesel rumbling next to me. Knowing myself to be a poor, weak, and burning fool, as well as a great, raging, and wonderful scribe, I pummeled the keys of my typewriter, and made the small Corona dance well into the morning. And always, the Tiger's purr was louder than the thunder of the keys.

NOT SINCE MARK TWAIN

And now you know why the Sage, at the end of my Pulitzer Prize winning play, *The Way the World Goes*, closes Act Three by saying, "The Tiger within whose name is love."

Gerald Hausman

A Rose for Charley

Hurricane Charley supplied me with a lot of ink and even a Best National Column Award for "Rose" -- but more than anything else, Charley gave me a sense of patience and courage in dealing with a natural disaster on its own terms. We stayed home for a category five with all of our animals -- Great Danes, Siamese cat, European Shorthair, Blue-Fronted Amazon Parrot, Dachshund and a host of unseen geckoes and Cuban tree frogs. Seems like the animals taught us more than we can ever repay: thanks to each and all, and especially to Charley, one of the worst hurricanes in U.S. history, for sparing us.

The day Hurricane Charley churned across Pine Island Sound and did a mad, destructive dance in Bokeelia, we were in our kitchen expecting the worst. From between the storm shutters, we peeked at the wind-whipped froth that sent bass from our pond hurtling through the air. Wingless bass flying through wind-bent, earth-pressed paperwood trees. No dream of life ever seemed more surreal. However, when Charley tired of sawing up slash pines, there came a dripping, dew-bright moment that was the eye of calm, the eye of false peace. Then after the ripping and the raging continued for a while, Charley seemed to get bored with woods wrecking and roof-pulling, and he spiraled out across Indian Field and then into Charlotte Harbor, whence he made his way, as everybody knows, to Punta Gorda.

We came out of our bolthole, blinking at the new world that lay before us.

It was indeed a brave new world, for which the phrase "wrath of Charley" has no significance. Mainly because it doesn't describe the haunted, unleaved, and in many cases, bare-barked trees. Or the canopies of vines woven into a tornadic tapestry that swung dreamily from the broken stalks of pines and palms.

A new world, yes. A wet and gleaming world that bore no resemblance to the Garden of Eden we'd shuttered off just two hours before when we locked and bolted ourselves into our house.

Miraculously the house still stood.

But it had taken a battering. Lorry and I, after counting our blessings, fell to that other preoccupation--counting our losses. This began with tropical trees, hand-planted so many years ago, to such things as shingles, soffit and fascia. The pool enclosure, so much a part of the house itself, was gone, much of it blown into our pond at the same time the bass were blowing out, most likely.

Anyway, it looked incongruous out there, like the spars of a black ship rising from the gloom of the green swamp.

I looked all around; nothing seemed familiar. Everywhere, rising from the plangent earth in ghosts of steam was the burnt, bruised fragrance of ripped roots and crushed leaves.

At last my eye fell on something known, something dear. A scraggly little rose bush that lived by our lanai. Its bony back was neither bent nor broken, and, unaccountably, there was one bright red-orange rose popping out among the purplish leaves.

"Hey," I cried out to Lorry, "here's a little guy unbeaten by Uncle Charley."

We stooped to admire the hardy little bush. Its brittle bark had been stripped clean of the lichen crusts that we'd been too busy to scrape off all summer.

In reverence, I touched the blossom, and it toppled lazily onto the ground. There was a sad second where I stared in disbelief. Then, turning away from sadness, I fetched the flower, and with a smile of hope, gave it to my wife.

She christened the flower, Hope, and put it in a crystal shot glass filled with water. And so we went about our lives that day, readying ourselves for the great indoor camping trip that would begin and end in our own house two weeks later.

During the day, however, I often spoke of the rose. How Charley had brought it forth. So, from destruction, creation. From bombs bursting to buds breaking. In *The Bhagavad-Gita*, the classic mystical work of ancient India there are these words of rapture that express what I was feeling.

You are the gods of wind,
death, fire, and water;
the moon; the lord of life;
and the great ancestor,
homage to you,
a thousand times homage!
I bow in homage to you
again and yet again.

That evening another miracle occurred: the phone rang. The power had been out since Charley's blue eye had gazed on Bokeelia. We were without power and water. In addition, the phone line—pinned down by fallen pines—was lying on the ground.

Therefore, we jumped when the phone rang.

I approached the receiver as I had the rose—gently. The sound as I pressed it to my ear was that of a hollow shell at the beach. A kind of *OM*. Then I heard the bright yet distant voice of Kelvin, our horticulturist friend from Trinidad.

No one knew the dark demon *Hurucan* better than Kelvin.

The first thing I said to him was, "How did you do that?"

"How did I do what?" he asked.

"Call us."

He laughed, then said, "I heard you were having a hurricane."

That seemed to say it all. Still, I was astounded.

"You got through," I murmured.

"Yes, mon," he assured me.

"How? Our phone's been dead."

"Love always gets through," he replied, as unsurprised by the munificence of his answer as I was overwhelmed by its beauty.

We went on, then, to talk about what had happened. How Charley had been a very bad boy. How our house had held up. How so many others had not. Kelvin was the perfect person to talk to after living through a category four. He'd been through a hundred tropical storms and who-knows-how many hurricanes. He was so reassuring, so respectful and yet amused, so endearing, so wonderful that I forgot the seriousness of what we were up against—the grim aftermath, the insurance woes, the broken parts of our home.

I didn't say a word about those things, though. Instead, I told Kelvin about the rose that bloomed in the midst of Charley's winds.

"Are there no more blossoms on it now?" he wondered.

"She gave us all she had, I think."

NOT SINCE MARK TWAIN

"No," Kelvin said, laughing. "You must go out there and tell that brave rose bush how much you love her, and how many more flowers you want to see her make."

"You mean that?"

Kelvin's laugh, because it's so deep and genuine, is infectious. I was laughing, too—for the first time since Charley. "Listen, my friend," Kelvin said, finally growing serious, "tell that *rose* how much you love her. Tell her, and she'll give you more blossoms."

"Is that how you do it in Trinidad?" I asked.

"We're in short supply of Miracle Grow, my brother. But there's no shortage of love here. There's lots of love in the things of this world."

"So you want me to speak to a rose bush."

"Yes, mon. "Tell her," he continued, "how brave she was facing that wind all by herself. Tell her—well, tell her whatever you want but let it come from the heart."

And with that, the phone went *zzzttt*, and then went dead.

In honor of our long-term friendship and Kelvin's infallible wisdom when it comes to the things of this world, I went directly outside into our ruined garden, and did what he'd told me to do.

As I stood in the ruined garden uttering praises, a heron flew over the pond. A warm glow flowed through me. I felt so grateful for being alive. And somehow, even after Charley, I was still in love with Pine Island. It seemed at that moment, the most enduring place on earth.

    The following day, we started to clean up.

    However, by day's grueling end, my wife and I were fumbling, tired, and hot. It was ninety two degrees in the shade. We were both staggering and the dog fence—so necessary in our yard with the Great Danes—was far from finished. I told Lorry, "I'm going inside to call the fence guy."

    She said, "With what phone? You know the line's dead."

    I sighed, and looked to the sky. It seemed like it was going rain.

    "Hey," she said, "We can do this."

    Then two red-shouldered hawks settled in a broken-off pine tree a few feet from us. They bobbed their heads, as if sighting something. Then they froze and gave us a red-eyed, sharp-beaked stare that went into our hearts. After which, in two divergent yet equally strident shrieks, the hawks screamed at us. Maybe they were sounding off about the dismal, dark state of the world, but at that moment, I didn't think so.

To me, it seemed, the hawks were talking to us.

    And, out of respect, we listened.

    They were such beautiful birds, a matched pair. Their shoulders were rusty-patched, each with a dark tail that had white bands on it. I'd never been this close to a red-shouldered hawk. After eyeing us and scolding us, both birds flew off, leaving the pine branch twanging behind them. Up into the Charley-polished air, the two hawks soared, and then, seemingly to underscore their message, they made a sharp and sudden descent, aimed in our direction. Each hawk fell in a series of perfectly turned, upside-down pirouettes. One roll after another, until, heading right for us, they broke off, singing that high song of angry triumph and crying despair.

I wiped the sweat from my eyes. Saying nothing, my wife and I finished fixing the fence. After seeing the hawks, we found silence more comforting than words. We just worked quietly and uncomplainingly until we were done. The fence, after we were finished with it, looked pretty good. Would it stand up to a galumphing Great Dane? We didn't care. But as we were walking back to the house with our tools, I said, "I think they were telling us to get back up and fight."

Lorry offered me a wry smile. "I think the lady hawk was saying we'd strung it up all wrong."

"That would be the male hawk, saying that," I told her.

"Not if they're like us," she replied.

This was an unfinished—and unfinishable—argument. No one wore the pants in our family, because neither one of us want to wear them.

That evening, like all others for the next two weeks, we bathed in our freshwater pond, and while we were paddling idly among the lily pads and amethyst lilies that encircle it, I saw a female anhinga drying its wings on the white trunk of a fallen paperwood tree. I knew this because of the bird's characteristic tan head and neck. Both males and females, however, have black bodies with white plumes and silver edgings on the wings. The anhinga, or snakebird as they're often called, sat in that emblematic pose--wings extended, head erect. Her pointed bill was yellow and straight, unlike the cormorant that has a descending, hooked beak.

She was so still she appeared sculptural. I swam close enough to gaze into her red-orange eye. Her sun-gilt feathers were the gleaming black gown of an Egyptian queen. Like the heron of the night before, here was another Pine Island blessing. I admired the anhinga as I treaded water among the lilies. I don't know if she admired me, but I know she tolerated me. I could feel that she wasn't afraid of me. Like the hawks, with whom we were somehow bonded, this ancestral relative gave us a sense of both timely and timeless confidence in the renewal of life.

"It seems like a time of beginnings," I said to Lorry. "Everything is destroyed, and yet reborn. Everything is known, and unknown. Nothing is timid or afraid. All things are what they are. Only one day ago, the creatures were as strangers. Now they are relations."

NOT SINCE MARK TWAIN

That evening as we lay in bed trying to fall asleep in the oppressive night heat, the only sound was the far off barking of a dog, the nearby roar of a generator, and the crazy riff of a displaced mockingbird that kept waking up and singing for no reason other than joyousness.

We couldn't sleep. A poem by Richard Wilbur kept filtering through my mind. Its title was "Love Calls Us to the Things of This World." It was a poem about angels—things all around us that speak to us in the language of poetry and praise.

I told Lorry, "Angels are animals and birds, too."

"Sometimes they are little rose bushes," she added.

I thanked each of the flowered, feathered, furred and finned. For it was their love of life that had called us to the things of this world, and awakened us to our own inner strength.

Gerald Hausman

Old Ben, Pam Snow, and the Blood of Summer

I wrote this one in 1993 and in 1995 it became part of a collection of stories Doctor Moledinky's Castle *shaped into what I called a "hometown novel." As a whole it was a novel, a memoir and a collection of short stories all rolled into one. It came and went and got good reviews.* School Library Journal *and a committee of librarians selected for SLJs 100 Children's Books Too Good to Miss list. I was proud but the book was gone. And yet it lived on because of this story about a boy, a girl and a chicken farmer named Ben. The story was so popular at schools when I'd tell it, or read it aloud, that one day I observed a very strange thing. I'd read it aloud in a cafetorium in northern Georgia and when I returned to my home in Florida, I read in an AP news story that a group of kids in that same town where I'd just been were arrested for hypnotizing chickens. The first hypno-chicken cult in America inspired by a short story. Wow. How many authors have that honor?*

Old Ben drove the school bus every day. He picked us up and let us out, and walked us to the door of our house while his bus idled in the road. One time, when my mom was late getting home from O'Connor's Market, Old Ben stayed parked in front of the house. He smoked his amber-grained Missouri meerschaum pipe, and we waited--about thirty of us--until she drove up into our driveway. And, do you know, that whole busload of kids just sat and talked, and there wasn't one fight or any kind of disorderly conduct. That was Old Ben for you. He seemed to cast a spell of kindness wherever he went, and within its embrace everyone was safe from harm.

One day, however all that changed--that was when Pam Snow came into our lives. But I'm getting ahead of myself again, aren't I?

Back to Old Ben: He had white hair, crinkly blue eyes, and skin brown as tanned pigskin. He was a heavyset man with a round, sad face, set off by big black bushy eyebrows. No one in Berkeley Bend was a good-natured as Old Ben; why he was friendly as sunshine 365 days of the year. We always wondered why he had no kids of his own, because he seemed to love children more than anything. His yard was always full of wild-eyed kids and redheaded chickens.

I used to like to chase after Old Ben's feisty little bantams, the ones that lay those perfect, pill-shaped eggs, so small and white and impossible to find. They ran around between my legs, dashing fast like fighters on quick springy muscular legs, with their heads bobbing and weaving as they eyed you up and down and tried to get out of your way.

The ducks though, were something else. They were never underfoot, but always nearby, floating like low-lying clouds and gabbing among themselves in duck-talk. Their eggs were everywhere, as if they had no particular use for them and they knew you were going to pick them up anyway.

On Fridays, all summer long, Old Ben killed chickens, plucked them clean, and sold them in town. That was the day Pauly and I waited for. We'd finish whatever chores we had around the house and run up in back of Bobby's house. Then run up across the road and behind Hilltop Garage, to the big field that went straight to Old Ben's farmhouse.

If it was Friday, Old Ben would be out in his yard, sharpening his axe on a large stone wheel. He had taken an old bicycle that we nicknamed "the death bike" and put a sharpening stone on the front. He would sit on the bicycle seat, whirring the pedals, while his hands pressed the axe against the spiraling stone. The sparks looped away like fireflies into the shady summer noon.

"Howdy, boys," Old Ben would say from the leather seat of the creaking, groaning death bike.

"Howdy, Old Ben," we'd chime.

"Come to watch the killin?" he'd ask innocently, his black brogan shoes circling beneath his bulk, whirling a low wind all around us. Those shoes were as much a part of Ben's image as his small-lipped smile. I guess you'd call them "Popeye boots," for that's what they looked like--great big balloon shoes that laced up tall. He kept them bright and shiny, and if a spot of dirt got on them, he quickly rubbed it off. When he walked, his brogans squeaked. Otherwise, for such a large man, he was quiet on his feet.

The bronze sparks nipped at our bare legs, tickling us. Pauly smiled with appreciation, and I smiled back. All week we'd waited for this moment. To us there was nothing morbid about it, the fact was, it was just plain fascinating.

"Well, I suppose this thing's sharp enough," Old Ben would finally say in his unaffected monotone voice. He got up out of the sharpener's seat and laid the axe in the bright green grass. Then he strolled toward the barn. We followed his snowy head into the tall, raftered darkness. Above our heads long blades of penetrating sunlight lay against the mounds of musty, dusty hay. Pigeons, hidden on the cross ties, cooed at our coming. The barn was much cooler than outside and the pigeon song was like cool water falling down on us from a great height.

Our job was to round up the stray chickens for Old Ben.

"The ones that are too hard to catch ain't ready to eat," Old Ben sighed up ahead as he fumbled around behind his tractor. I flushed a blustery little bantam, who made good his escape out the door.

After a little while Old Ben caught a few; and then a few more. He dropped them into a burlap bag, and we held the bag shut while he went inside and fetched his Jew's harp. This was a ceremony with him, and for us a free symphony. We sat out in the yard, waiting for Old Ben to return.

Pretty soon he came out, a-twanging. "Dere-de-de-dere," the plucky harp went, and Ben rolled to and fro, like a circus bear trained for tricks. And the bear's grin was on his lips, as if savoring some old sweet sticky memory of honey.

"What's that do?" Pauly asked the first time Ben ever invited us to a killin in his yard.

"What, the harp?" Old Ben shook his wintry head, laughing deep in his chest. His belly bulged, shook up and down. And his small eyes, like green-bottle glass, twinkled in the sun.

"Why, Pauly, don't you know the setup? First, the music -- to soothe 'em. Then, the belly scratchin' -- to set them up. Then, the killin', to let them off and finish the job."

That was how he did it.

A ceremony that made me think that the chickens knew it by heart; knew just what the deal was, and had, long ago, agreed to it.

After Old Ben twanged at the chickens in the bag to soothe them, he took them out by the feet. By then, they were all blinky, wondering what was going on, but not really afraid or anything. Then Old Ben laid them out, side by side, and scratched their tummies. One by one, each and every chicken fluffed out and went fast asleep. If you've never seen it done, maybe you can't imagine it: chickens all puffed out like pillows, snoozing in the midday sun.

Then Old Ben scooped them up, still sound asleep, and

NOT SINCE MARK TWAIN

one by one he chopped off their heads.

Now, the moment the axe fell, the real magic happened -- the thing that we'd waited for all week long. No, it wasn't the killin, so much as the second part. I don't know what name to give, except maybe the revivin, though nobody called it that but me.

Anyway, those dead headless chickens sprang back up on their springy little feet and made a run for the woods. naturally our job -- Pauly's and mine -- was to catch them. So we went chasing after these dead chickens . . .

They didn't get far, but any distance gained by a dead chicken is pretty far where I'm concerned. As I was saying, the chickens would shoot off the chopping block, alert and alive and full of vigor, and head for the woods, running this way and that, with Pauly and me hurrying after them. One time one actually got away from us and we never saw it again. Old Ben said a fox probably got it. But every night for weeks we had scary dreams about that headless chicken roaming the back woods.

Well, that was Friday and Old Ben and the killin.

We never thought anyone else knew about Old Ben's chicken killin, but one Friday morning when Pauly went out of town with his parents, I was riding my bike past Pam Snow's house, and she waved and asked me over.

"Where are you headed in such a hurry?" Pam Snow asked, her grey eyes widening with interest.

I flipped down my kickstand and caught my breath. One look at those dazzling eyes and the potato chip fiasco came back full force.

I pushed the disastrous chip out of my mind. "I'm heading up to Ben's," I told her. "It's Friday, chicken killin day."

"Can I come?"

She asked so innocent and nice, I forgot to answer no, because chicken killin' is not for people like Pam Snow. But she caught me off balance and I heard myself say: "Why not?"

"Can I ride with you?" she cooed.

"Why not?" I said again (dumb).

She got on sideways. I raised the kickstand and began to pedal down the road, behind Sleazy Joe's Garage, across the field to Old Ben's. By the time we got there Ben had already done the bagging.

"You're late," he commented, unsmiling.

"What's he doing?" Pam Snow whispered.

"He sings to the chickens first," I told her knowingly.

"Oh, no," Old Ben said. His face was stern, the summer glitter gone from his eyes. I'd never seen him look like that.

"Pam's all right," I said. "She's not afraid of anything."

Ben's usually smiling face had "no" written all over it.

Shaking his head, "What would your mother think, he muttered, "nice girl like you seeing a chicken killin." It wasn't a question; more like a statement of fact.

"She doesn't care," Pam Snow said softly. Her voice was pigeony, and calm. Perfectly calm, almost disinterested.

"Well -- I care." Ben backed off, his voice trailing.

"I want to see," Pam Snow said earnestly.

"What girl wants to see blood splashing around," Old Ben remarked darkly. Again, not a question.

"I do," Pam Snow said. There was a sudden violet light in her eyes, something that suggested a little more than mere interest. If I hadn't known her better, I would've imagined there was malice in those eyes. But I knew Pam better than that -- at least I thought I did.

Old Ben's eyebrows rose, lowered. He turned, stepped closer to Pam Snow, looking at her inquisitively.

"You want to see blood and gore?" he asked, his black eyebrows raised high under his tan, wrinkled brow.

Pam Snow smiled, nodded pleasantly. Her calm eyes were trained on Old Ben's, and she didn't look away.

Then he turned and went to the death bike. He reached in the grass for his axe, ran his big brown thumb over the edge. Plucking a hair from his head, Old Ben put the blade to it -- and, I swear, that white hair split in two.

Pam Snow gave a cooey little laugh, but her lips hardly moved at all.

Old Ben shrugged. Sighing, he said, "All right, so be it!" He went inside the house and got his harp.

"He's going to do it," I whispered confidently.

"I know." Pam Snow smiled. Once again I saw her eyes brighten and darken under the shade trees. Perhaps it was only my imagination, but in the quiet shadows of Ben's sleepy yard, I thought her eyes changed color. As I looked at them, they seemed to turn to a shade of plum, dark and hidden, and not friendly.

A moment later Old Ben started twanging on the Jew's harp. It didn't sound like it usually did; the notes were kind of somber.

He twanged.

I heard more cooing, but was afraid to look.

Then he took the drowsy chickens out of the bag and scratched their tummies, and they were all asleep. There was more cooing. And I felt a hand, cold as buttermilk fresh from the fridge, fit into my own.

I held my breath. I had her hand in mine. A tickly feeling traveled through me. I shivered briefly, and felt her hand grow heavier.

Old Ben placed the first chicken on the stump. Its eyes were wide open, staring dreamily into space. I saw one of its legs move very, very slowly.

The bright axe winked in the sunlight, rose, and lowered.

Pam Snow's hand closed tightly.

The dead chicken jumped from the chopping block to

the ground and ran off into the summer air, flopping its wings.

My feet were numb, leaden; my hand was riveted by hers. I dared not move, hardly drew breath -- waiting.

Then my hand was free, empty and open.

I saw someone dashing after the headless chicken. Standing stock-still, I looked at Ben. He shrugged. "Can't tell . . . with women . . . sometimes," he said under his breath.

Pam Snow ran through the sun and shadow chasing the chicken.

Old Ben shook his head, watching. The small bear's smile was back. Sweat trickled down his forehead. The air felt hot and thick, and for the first time it smelled of rank feathers and warm blood.

We watched her walking serenely through the cool shade, carrying the chicken by the wings. It seemed unnatural. Pauly and I always carried them by the legs.

I looked away.

Ben did too. Then he wiped the sweat off his brow.

"Well, that's it for the day. Looks like rain, don't it?"

I nodded. It surely did. But before he got his axe wiped off and put away in the barn, and the dreaming chickens were back awake, Pam Snow had disappeared.

"Where'd that girl go to?" he asked me. "Looked away for a spell and she was gone."

We looked at the chopping block where she'd placed the

runaway. The wings were folded out in a grotesque manner. The neck of the chicken was dripping dark purple blood.

I felt my stomach roll.

Old Ben said only one thing after that. First he stooped down, picked up the dead chicken, and toted it by the feet into the house. Then he turned to me and said: "I don't care who you bring next time, Bud, but see to it they don't go stealing chicken heads." It was the first time he'd ever called me Bud.

Biking home, I felt sick to my stomach. In my mind, the purple blood was drip-drip-dripping on the grass, and the day was somehow spoiled. But I didn't -- and couldn't quite -- understand why.

At the same time, I kept remembering the way Pam Snow's hand felt in mine, as if it belonged there.

I was afraid I would never hold it again.

My mind went spinning around like the sharpening stone on Old Ben's death bike. Around and around.

What had happened? I wasn't sure that I knew.

There was Pam Snow's hand, soft as a snowflake, melting.

There was the blood of summer spilling on the leaves.

There was that look of veiled violet in Pam Snow's eyes; I saw it again now as my mind went on whirling. She had liked it, hadn't she? The blood, the killin time. And suddenly I knew what was wrong with me. For Pauly and me, those chickens running headless through the woods were almost dreamlike, something that happened but was hardly real; it couldn't be, for the dead don't walk.

In one swift moment I knew that Pam Snow's presence in Old Ben's killin yard had made the whole thing real, very real. The purple blood would be spattered on those leaves forever. And so would her snowflake hand always be melting in mine as the summer leaves burned green as candles in the hot light of day.

Gerald Hausman

Yarns and Tales

NOT SINCE MARK TWAIN

Rattlesnake Pete, Goiter Healer

When I am asked how I get stories, how I find them, I often say, "They are given." But people don't always believe that. They want to imagine that I do something beyond the ordinary; that I acquire the story through some mischief or madness, some type of necromancy or magic. Usually the mischievous one is the storyteller, not the listener whose ever fiber is bent on getting the words down the way they were said. Well, anyway -- I have to admit people do come out of nowhere and tell me their stories -- in airports, on the street, and even in emails. The following tale is one of those "givens."

The man sitting next to me in the hotel lobby leans over and says, "You look like Rattlesnake Pete... are you?"

I shake my head. "Who's he?"

"See this here goiter I got on my neck?"

There is a lump on the left side of his throat.

"Well, sir, the man says, "Rattlesnake Pete, he cured it. But after a while it grew back. Need another cure. But Pete's long gone by now. That was in nineteen-hundred and . . . I forget." The man tents
 his eyes with his fingers.

We are in The Hampton Inn and I walk over to the coffee bar and get a refill. "You want one?" I ask the goiter guy.

"Black," he says. "Thanks."

I pour two black coffees and return to the enormous open lounge that had so many sofas the place looked like a car lot. There was a big stain on the sea blue carpet where someone had fallen asleep with a mug of coffee. I enjoy the stain, perhaps because it looks so Rorschach and I can look at it and see an arabesque of owls, a tango of whales. Very dreamlike -- like the car lot. Like the goiter guy.

Like the darkening winter sky.

Flakes coming down. One at a time.

I like this; we don't see much snow in South Florida.

"So you were saying." I hand my new friend a white ceramic mug of black coffee.

One sip and he starts right in. "Rattlesnake Pete's real name's Peter Gruber, in case you want to look him up. Never can tell when you're going to have a goiter."

He pauses to watch the lazy flakes drift down from that menacing steely sky. As he stares outside, I stare, very briefly, at the swelling on his neck which is about as big as a baby's fist. He swings back abruptly, catches my glance.

"I see you looking. It's all right. Everybody does. That thing was as big as a small football." He pauses for a moment, searching my eyes for surprise. "Bout like this." He rounds his hands, holds held them six inches apart.

I nod, sip my coffee. "That's good size--"

"Nah," he says, cutting me off. "Big ones are so large they look like a second head growing out of your neck." He winks. Then he reaches into the top pocket of his plaid woolen shirt and takes out a handkerchief. The man blows his nose like a trumpet. People in the lobby turn their heads.

"This is how he did it," the man says, stuffing his handkerchief back into his top pocket. "Right here--" he pats the lump on his neck. "Rattlesnake Pete put his biggest, fattest rattler, and that thing coiled up around your neck so it felt like it was choking you to death. Pete's game was to wrap the reptile round the goiter."

"Then what happened?"

The man's eyes widen. Eyebrows arching, he explains. "Why, he'd let the snake squeeze the devil out of that goiter and just when you thought you was going die, Pete'd uncoil the reptile, and all the while it was rattling to beat the band, then he'd kiss it on the head and put it away in the back room. You believe me, don't you?"

"Sure do. Hey, that's some story."

"Only it ain't a story, it's the truth," he states. "You know, old Pete kept a corpse in the back room. That thing was dug out of the earth of the Cardiff Giant. He'd show you some of these things, if you wanted to see them. He had the last cigar of the last man executed in the electric chair in the state of New York, and he had a hairless cow from India and the bald, bare skull of Sheridan's Civil War horse. But the best thing about Pete, he had twenty nine rattlesnake bites, four copperhead bites, and the biggest mustache you ever saw. Old Pete was a simple soul with a seedy saloon and the rattlesnakes and the corpse from the dirt of Cardiff – oh, that's right, I already told you that."

For a moment, we watch the snowflakes at the window and I am about to say, "How beautiful" when he says, "What a mess."

"Guess it depends where you're from."

"No, it don't. Going to be some nasty pile-ups out there today." He says this with a fatal look in his eye.

I turn the subject back to Pete. "Did Pete's cure always work?"

"Some say yes; some say no. I'm in the yes group. This thing here dropped down to the size of a peanut, like this--" His right forefinger and thumb made as if to pinch a peanut.

"And then what happened?"

"Grew back. Had to take another cure."

"And how about *now*?"

"Pete's gone somewheres. Ain't no cures like that anymore. People're too smart for their own good, nowadays." He sighs noisily, scratches the side of his head. "Come to think of it, it's all part of the cure."

"What is?"

"You know, seeing all them things in that back-of-the-bar museum. I'd like to have a leaf off that cigar the deadman smoked, a bit of dirt from corpse of the Cardiff Giant, some little bit of skin off that stony lady corpse, and maybe one tiny little hair off that hairless cow from India --"

"What about a splinter of bone from Sheridan's horse?" I added.

"That, too, yes, sir."

"And what would you do with them -- if you had them?"

He blinks. "Don't know . . . exactly." He rubs his eyes, and heaves himself to a standing position.

From where I sit, looking up, the goiter is larger. It seems to have grown.

He meets my gaze, winks, says, "It does that sometimes."

"Does what?"

"Gets smaller. Whenever I tell that story, it shrinks a little. You see, telling is part of the cure, just like when Pete took me round to see them oddities. What I need's a good big rattlesnake," he says, grinning.

"But I won't be able to do that until after snowmelt."

Then the man turns and walks off, and the farther he gets from me the smaller the goiter looks until I can barely see it, and by then he's out the door into the snowstorm.

Gerald Hausman

I turn back to the coffee stain on the floor, but now all I see are goiters.

NOT SINCE MARK TWAIN

Sam

It was in Biloxi, Mississippi that I heard a "realistic" mermaid tale told by my friend James Clois Smith Jr.. Then, in Jamaica, in the 1980s, I heard another spin on the same myth. Both of these were tucked away in my memory for future use. Then I read J.D. Suggs' story of how he was kidnapped by a mermaid and the three stories merged into one. I soon found that audiences of all ages liked to hear "Sam" read aloud. It's a good yarn for the road, that old forgotten sea road of long ago.

Before they had motors, ships traveled about with steam. And before that they had sails, as you know.

There were mermaids in those days, and they followed the ships. If you called anybody's name, the mermaid would ax for it—"Give it to me."

If you didn't give it to them, they would capsize the ship. So the captain had to change all the men's names. One was named Hatchet and another was named Ax. One was Hammer, and another, Furniture.

Whenever the captain wanted a man to do something, he said, "Hammer, go on deck and look out."

Then the mermaid would say, "Give me Hammer." So they throwed a hammer overboard, and the ship was allowed to proceed on. Another time the captain might say, "Ax, you go down in the kindling room, start a fire in the boiler, it's going dead." But the mermaid overhears it, and she says, "Give me Ax." So they throw her an iron ax.

Next day captain says, "Suit of Furniture, go down in the state room and make up those beds." And the mermaid says, "Give me Suit of Furniture," so they throwed a whole suit of furniture overboard.

Now, one day captain made a mistake, he forgot himself, and said, "Sam. Go in the galley and cook supper." The mermaid heard that and she said, "Oh, give me Saaammm!"

But they didn't have nothing on that ship that was named Sam, so they had to throw Sam overboard.

Soon as Sam hit the water, the mermaid grabbed him.

Then she blew a bubble over his head, so he could breathe. Her hair was so long, she wrapped Sam up and he didn't even get wet, and that's how she took him to her home at the bottom of the sea.

When they get there, the mermaid unwraps Sam, and has a good look at him. "OH, Sam, you sure do look nice," she says.

"Then she says, "Do you like fish?"

Now Sam loved to eat fish most every night, but he was smart, so he said, "No, I won't even cook a fish if captain asks me."

NOT SINCE MARK TWAIN

Says the mermaid, "Well, then—should we get married, Saaammm?"

And Sam shrugs, and as he doesn't have nothing better to do he says, "I guess."

So they were married.

But after a while Sam begins to step out with other mermaids down there in the deeps. This got his wife jealous, so she went after Sam's girlfriend and gave her a good beating. And she didn't show up no more, but one day the girlfriend saw Sam, and said to him, "Would you like to go back home to dry land?" And Sam can't help it, he's powerful homesick, and he says without thinking, "Yes, I would." And that girlfriend grabs him up and wraps him up and ferries him to dry land.

And do you know what that mean mermaid says?

She says, "Now if he can't do me no good, he sure can't do her no good neither." And away she goes with a little flip of the tail.

So Sam got back to where he was before he shipped out to sea, and he told everyone about his great adventures under the ocean and his life there, and he told of the things he saw, and how the mermaids had purple lips and greenish seaweed color hair. And all the land women went out and demanded purple lipstick and green hair dye, and that's why we see so much foolery like that today— all because of Sam.

Gerald Hausman

The Biggest Barracuda

Once, while telling this story in St. Petersburg, Florida, a lady came up to me and asked if the man I called Dana lived most of the year in Marsh Harbour in the Bahamas. I said, "Yes, same guy." She said, "I've seen his butt and it was shark bit." People like veracity in stories and I usually try to give them that. Sometimes I get carried away. Not long ago a boy in Tampa raised his hand after I'd told a story and said, "How do we know if you're telling the truth?" "You don't," I replied. That said, I beg you to believe this one because it happened just like this. If you don't believe me, ask Dana.

I went out my backdoor every day, took a step, and there was the great big blue Caribbean sea as near as my nose and far as the distant horizon. Nothing between me and the reef except fine-particled sand and that famous gin clear water. Beyond the crystal shallows, the mysterious purple beginnings of depths. Cerulean blue. Magenta. Blue, blue depths dropping to a famous place called the "horns of the bull" because of the curve of the reef and the breakers bone white shine. Out there, fish twinkled in the velvety gloom. Overhead glassy calm, but just below this the current pulled towards Haiti. The burnt orange sea fans hung on the edge of the cliff of reef. I'd sometimes watch them as the tide frosted white over my skin, bathing me in a snowstorm of tiny, tickly bubbles.

Mostly I liked to stay within the reef where it was quieter and safer.

Day after day I skimmed the sandy bottom, frightening flounder and watching them flutter away in a vapor trail of sand. Sometimes I scared myself when a stingray shot out from under me, and then, heart pounding, I'd watch it wing itself away into the grape-colored distance. Occasionally a squadron of squid hung luminous in front of my face, their wise and intelligent eyes surmising my intentions. The backdrop was misty violet, and below that, there were acres of turtle grass, dancing to and fro in the pulsation of the current.

I wasn't prepared for the barracuda. It came out of nowhere and while we seemed to see each other at the same time, I knew from experience that it had been watching me.

This was no ordinary guy, let me tell you -- this was a venerable hunter, a reef prowler who'd been around many a year.

It took me several seconds to comprehend the animal's size; it was at least ten feet from toothy mouth to swallow-finned tail.

Seeing this monster reminded me of Dana, my diving buddy who'd been bitten by a lemon shark. The shark wanted the grouper Dana had just speared. After circling him once or twice, the lemon shark bumped Dana hard, turned him around, and then took a big bite out of his butt. Dana was fat, and heavy. But that didn't stop him from shooting out of the water like a missile. Once airborne, Dana, ran on his flippers – on the top of the water – for about five feet. Then he flopped into the dinghy. The lemon shark stayed behind only because it got what it wanted – Dana's red grouper.

Barracudas, as any diver will tell you, are unpredictable.

This beast was larger than the one that ripped another friend's dive mask -- and in doing so, the flesh of his face -- over at Reef Pointe.

This guy was much larger.

I looked at my hands.

My stomach turned to ice.

I was wearing all of my turquoise rings – all five of them -- and they were flashing prettily in the sun.

Noticing this, I quickly used my thumb to roll the rings around so that the bright blue stone faced down. But the sun caught the silver and there was nothing I could do about that.

The great fish eased slowly near. But oddly, it turned and was lengthwise again. It seemed to me the fish wanted me to see how long it was, how dangerous it was, how it had me.

If it wanted me.

I was in deep water, slogging with my fins. My snorkel was just at the surface and I was drawing deep draughts of air, trying not to let my heart beat so infernally fast.

Barracudas can hear heartbeats.

Hanging there, close to the reef, I had few choices.

Rise like Dana, walk on water? That was just a story, even though I'd seen the row of perfect spaced magenta marks all the way down his right, white, butt cheek.

Fleeing was out of the question.

Curiously, the night before I read a magazine article about a boy who was badly chomped by a bull shark. The animal thumped up on the sand, rolled over and severed the boy's legs off at the knees. I pressed my mental delete button, got rid of that image.

Another took its place, all in a matter of seconds.

Same magazine, different story. Man faces grizzly bear on lonely mountain trail. Bear comes galloping for him. Man's wearing ski coat that makes him appear bigger than he is. Man puffs himself up, puts his arms out, spreads his legs – looks large. Bear throws on brakes, gravels to a stop. Looks puzzled. "Hey, that's not the little bit of cheese I saw." Grizzlies have bad eyes. This one wandered off, coughing and woofing disgruntlement.

Now the barracuda came closer.

I saw its sleek, silver torpedo length. The barra's eye was bright as a moon and his under-bite was all spike teeth. His uppers gleamed.

Monster.

The ancient scars on his sunny sides told me this guy was a battler. I felt his hunger. His eye studied every swipe of my fins, for nothing else on me, or about me, was moving.

I visualized a storm of red bubbles and blood swirls.

He'd saw me apart in two seconds.

Strangely, seeing my imminent death inspired me.

I tried the only trick I had.

Opened my arms, spread my legs for bear.

Hung myself to dry in the coral-headed, daylit current; and waited.

I had air – a lungful of snorkel breath.

My stomach was bellied out like a fat man.

Belly pushing triggers certain internal functions.

Out came a thunder mother of a fart -- a great fatman fart that sent up a chain of bells.

Startled, the barracuda soared away into the dark blue gloom.

But not before turning his great length the other way as he shot off towards a hole in the reef.

As he made a knifelike quarter turn, I glimpsed the side of him he'd kept from me.

The barracuda was a one-eye.

Like me, hiding my fear of him, he'd tried to keep something from me. The killer could only see on one side of his head.

NOT SINCE MARK TWAIN

Well, we were both fakers, and so, lived to see another day.

And the moral of the story?

Don't hold back what's inside, it might save your life.

Don't go farting around either.

Neither moral holds up that much.

Maybe the real moral is, read more.

Gerald Hausman

The Seventh Bridle

The Seventh Bridle is a found story but, right now, I can't for the life of me remember where I got it -- picked it up on the road somewhere in Kentucky, Ohio, Virginia, Iowa, or all of these places. It's a just-for-fun story that would easily make a good folksong and maybe already is. I've read it aloud in horse country through the deep south and into Texas, and naturally, people love it there. Unpublished but not unheard.

I woke up in my rocking chair in front of the fire at the stroke of midnight! In the dim light I saw six men digging under my hearthstone. These are men I'd seen before on Scrag Mountain, but what are they doing in my cabin?

I watched a while, and they got my hearthstone up and fetched seven bridles out from under it. These they took outside. I followed behind them softly. Then the six men bridled up six of my best red calves, and they galloped off into the night. I saw them thunder off under the oaks, and then, to my surprise, they flew up into the air, and sailed out off into the sky.

Then I saw, down at my feet a seventh bridle just a-laying there on the grass. So I picked it up and I tried it on one of my calves to see if the magic would work for me as well.

NOT SINCE MARK TWAIN

Well, sir, that calf bolted and blew and took off like a deer and we half-flew and half-rode all the way down to Coffee Creek. There the calf jumped the crick, and the bridle slipped off. That calf, head held high, struck the water with its hoofs and thrashed around while I got a good soaking myself.

Pretty soon, while I was trying to stay afloat, along come a big oak limb. I clumb on top and got myself situated. I was safe. And I still had a good grip on that bridle, too. But just as I got comfy on that there log, I pass under a big water hickory, and from off a limb above my head, a large blue mountain cat drops down.

I stared at the cat; and the cat stared at me. And then when I was a-looking into its red-ember eyes, darned if that crazy animal didn't jump on me and grab the bridle outten my hand, and plug the bit right into my mouth, and ride off the log with me as its mount.

Away I go, this time a-swimming and a-galloping up into the milky clouds where I spun around at the cat's whim and desire until it reined me and sent me shooting down to earth like a comet. Forthwith, it tied me up in front of a cave mouth, and then it went inside.

Now, as a thinking man, which I am, or leastwise was, I got to thinking: If I could just spit that bridle out, I'd be okey-dokey again. But I couldn't manage to do it by the time that fool cat come out of the cave and stepped up for another ride. I let him get closer, and then---Fwhoosh!—I spat the bridle out, and worked it into the cat's mouth, and went off for a ride on his back the same way he'd rid me.

We pummeled the earth for quite a good while over trees and hills and hollers. And we didn't quit that ride until the sun come up. After which I unbridled the cat, and he went to sleep under a persimmon tree. I don't think he ever woke up. But I unbridled him and hung that thing up in my barn. Lord knows, I never wanted to see what would happen if I used it again.

Well, human beings is curious, you know. And one day some years later I got to wondering what would happen to my old plow mule if I bridled him with that there bridle in the barn. So, one day I slid that thing into his mouth, and...he turned into a beautiful Tennessee Walker, all glossy and pretty, and you know something, he's stayed that way, too.

You may as well ask, everybody does—What happened to that bridle? Well, I burned it. But my Tennessee plow mule didn't turn back into a mule. No, sir, he's still the best Tennessee Walker that ever trod the earth.

Y'all come over sometime, and try him out!

NOT SINCE MARK TWAIN

Of Lions and Men

A few years ago I was at a conference telling stories to young people and during a break I went outside the school with Cherokee storyteller Gayle Ross to get a breath of fresh Texas Gulf Stream air and out of the oak trees comes a man in painter's pants and with splotches of white paint on his shirt, and he asks us if we are storytellers and we say yes and he says, "I am too...would you like to hear one of mine?" and we say yes and out comes this story, and that's exactly what happened and he said I could tell it but he didn't want me to sing it because that's what he did. So a little cuento from the borderlands, unsung, and for the first time, writ.

There was once a lion who fell in love with a girl.

"I love your long dark hair," the lion said.

"I'm sorry but I am already promised to another," the girl said. She had no wish to marry a lion, besides what she said was true – she was already promised.

The lion thought to himself – in the grand manner of lions – how could a mere man compete with me?

Gently, he continued his courting -- "I would care for you like no man; and I would love you like a lion."

"I see what you are," said the girl. Then, wary of the lion's teeth and claws, she added, "I'll think about it."

"Very well," said the lion, and in his heart there was hope.

Yet when the girl told her grandmother what had happened, the old woman told her, "You cannot marry a lion."

"What shall I tell him then?"

"Tell the lion he must file his teeth and cut his nails," the old woman said cleverly.

"—And what good will that do?" the girl questioned.

"A lion will *never* agree to such a thing," the grandmother answered.

The following day, the girl saw the lion and said, "I would like you to file your teeth and cut your nails."

The lion was surprised at this request, but thinking about it, he said, "After filing and cutting – we can marry?"

The girl nodded.

The lion ran his long claws through his thick mane, and said, "If that is your wish, that is what I shall do."

The girl hastened away.

At home, the girl told her grandmother – "The lion has agreed. Now what should I do?"

The grandmother frowned. "A lion would *never* do that."

"—But… what if he *did?*"

"Then you will have to tell him, once again, that you are promised to another."

The following day the girl saw the lion and he looked altogether different.

"I have complied with your request," the lion said. He seemed resigned but not terribly sad.

"You are less of a lion," the girl said, "but I still can't marry you."

"Why?" the lion asked.

"Well, you see, it is as I said once before, I am promised to another."

At that, the lion lost his temper. "You've tricked me," he growled. His lip curled. He showed his sawed-off teeth and flexed his missing claws.

"You can't hurt me," the girl said. "And I still can't marry you."

The lion, angry though he was, burst into tears. "I may be without my teeth," he said, "and I may be without my claws, but I still have my heart, and now it is broken."

The girl slept peacefully that night, but the lion did not sleep at all. He roved the meadows and moaned and he never got over his broken heart.

And that is why lions and men have something in common.

Gerald Hausman

The Logger Who Knew Mark Twain

"You think because I have just one arm
I can't drive? You think because I'm illiterate
I don't know Mark Twain? Well I do, or did,
he was grumpier and meanern'me."

One switchback after another, he rattles on.
"Watch the road," I tell him.
"What for?" he shouts.

Acknowledgements

Gulfshore Life Magazine of Naples, Florida for allowing me to use the following from my column Pine Island Soundings -- *Along Came Bob Washington; A Tree Frog Named Houdini; The Parrot's Scribe; The Ancient Itch; A Rose for Charley.*

New Mexico Magazine for *Talking Adobe*

Greenwillow/HarperCollins for *Open Water Swimming*

E.P. Dutton *for Snail*

Daw Books for *Tyger, Tyger Purring Loud*

Simon & Schuster for *Old Ben, Pam Snow and the Blood of Summer*

Gerald Hausman

ABOUT THE AUTHOR

Gerald Hausman, author of over 70 books, has traveled widely in America as a professional storyteller and public speaker. His work in Native American studies has been aired on radio coast-to-coast and cited in *The New York Times* and many other national and international publications. Mr. Hausman has received 35 awards and honors from the American Folklore Society; Bank Street College; New York Public Library; National Council of Social Studies; Parents Choice; Children's Book Council; Society for the Prevention of Cruelty to Children for his books, some of which have been adapted for film, many of which have been used in classrooms around the world. His collection of Native American origin stories, *How Chipmunk Got Tiny Feet*, has reached over one million readers and his numerous books about Bob

Marley, co-authored by Cedella Marley, have been reprinted each year since the 1990s. Mr. Hausman has been called "a native of the world" by teachers and educators in all walks of life.

Made in the USA
Columbia, SC
14 November 2017